ON NEUTRAL ZONES

On Neutral Zones

A novella
by

DANIEL FALATKO

BOOKS

Adelaide Books
New York / Lisbon
2020

ON NEUTRAL ZONES
A novella
By Daniel Falatko

Published by Adelaide Books, New York / Lisbon
adelaidebooks.org

Editor-in-Chief
Stevan V. Nikolic

For any information, please address Adelaide Books
at info@adelaidebooks.org
or write to:
Adelaide Books
244 Fifth Ave. Suite D27
New York, NY, 10001

ISBN: 978-1-952570-56-8

Printed in the United States of America

A panic normalized long ago.

Struggling to push through one of the five rotating glass doors at Smart Sani-Saver headquarters at ten-minutes-past-five. Already the masses were seeping out of the buildings lining 3rd Avenue, a grey and black business casual army being suctioned north into the grand, grizzled mouth of Grand Central. He fell into step as he always did, his heels aching with the impact of hot concrete through the soles of worn-down dress shoes.

He had forgotten to load the dishwasher that morning. This made the 5:35 train an absolute must. Checking his phone, he had plenty of time. Still there was no way to slow his steps. Even the slightest ease-up in pace would cause those marching behind him to quickly overtake him. The force of their advance, hundreds deep, tripped down and stamped out right there on the Avenue in broad daylight. They wouldn't be able to mop up his blood until long after rush hour had passed.

A screaming match between a Lyft driver and yellow cab driver had caused gnarled car traffic up ahead, rendering the intersection at 40th an impassible mass of jostling pedestrians and motionless cars glaring in the intense late afternoon sun. A crescendo of blaring horns. This is why he found himself moving west on 39th that day. He never took this route. Storefronts he did not recognize. Buildings he had never seen before, their architectures jagged and mismatched.

An alien hellscape. An unplanned detour into a foreign zone. This must have been why he was looking up at that particular moment, why his senses were on higher alert than usual. On 40th Street he would have been walking with his head down, concentrating on the rhythm of his feet on the sidewalk. His only thoughts would be on the familiar obstacles separating him from his present place and a seat upon the 5:35 train. On 39th Street this strategy just wasn't effective. The obstacles were now obscure. He scanned over the heads of the rushing factions before him, zeroing in on every fresh, terrifying detail.

It was from this jagged palette that his salvation emerged. It came in the form of three white, lowercase letters set against a black modernist overhang spilling over the front entrance of an otherwise standard pre-war building. The letters seemed obscenely out of place within that muted grey netherworld, stamped in small font and gleaming like polished teeth floating in a rain puddle.

pod

The insults and threats started coming almost immediately.

"Hey dick, it's called a side*walk*."

"Move it, asshole."

"I'll fucking kill you."

His knees nearly buckled. His heart kicked cruelly at his ribcage. He had to concentrate hard just to remain afloat in the stampede. A wounded swimmer. Though his pace had slowed, he allowed the pedestrian current to sweep him toward shore. It wasn't until he reached Grand Central that he had the chance to stand still for a moment, tucked into a corner by the shoeshine stands. This is an interesting development, he thought, all panicked and worn thin at the sight of three random letters on an unfamiliar street. I need to get myself together here if I'm going to make that 5:35. Across the corridor a homeless men sitting atop a massive bag of plastic bottles eyed him with interest. Will you be joining us, his gaze seemed to ponder.

"Not just yet," he said out loud, causing one of the shoeshine man to look up from his phone.

A deep breath, a straightening of the posture, and he walked off toward his train as if everything hadn't changed.

It was a scene he had witnessed well over a thousand times. The upper reaches of the Bronx fading into a series of neutral post-industrial zones, before the suburbs really gain traction. Half the time he wouldn't even watch this scenery, focusing on his phone or an iPad or half reading a PowerPoint printout while obsessing on 401Ks, mortgage payments, tuition funds, History Channel schedules. The times he would look out the window he would do so with a specific purpose, checking the skies for signs of rain or seeing if it was still snowing. But he never focused. He never really watched the scenery.

On that day he did watch. He observed everything he could from the 125th Street station all the way to his stop. He watched as the neatly packed buildings and logical, condensed grids of Harlem, Upper Manhattan, and the Bronx gave way to wide swaths of empty lots, lost streets with little planning or logic behind them, strip malls and massive buffet eateries. He watched as it all distilled to a greener vision of lawns and trees and public parks, temporarily lush spaces practically begging for the desolation of winter. All wasted space. Inefficient and uncontrolled.

Placing his forehead against the glass, he closed his eyes and tried his best to breathe.

They make cars so boxy these days. He was thinking this as he searched for his own boxy vehicle within the expansive commuter lot. He knew the general area where he usually parked, so he began hitting the "unlock" button on his keychain as he weaved between misshapen Subarus and Tauruses until he heard two beeps. He was thinking he should place a bumper sticker or decal on the back so he could identify it more easily, but on the short drive to his house he realized he had no idea what type of sticker he would want.

Intrusive thoughts kept coming at him with a regimented intensity. He considered how inconvenient and frightening it was just to own a vehicle. The costs involved. Both financial and psychic. Such easy access to death. What was happening to him that afternoon? The winds must have been strange. Perhaps his sugar intake had been higher than usual. Maybe it was the setting of the season. Summer clamping down. A Tom Petty song he had always enjoyed came ringing out on Classic FM.

He switched off the radio.

The single white turret on the front of his house had always been a point of great pride. It gave the small structure a castle-like vibe. Pausing to observe the turret on the traffic-less street as he always did. On that day it struck him as silly and excessive, a fierce horn adorning the head of an otherwise weak animal. Looking away quickly, embarrassed, he pulled into the driveway with an unfamiliar but satisfying screech of rubber.

Catharine was not yet home. The most fortunate of breaks. He made a move for the dishwasher, passing through a hallway with polished wood floors and a doorway with a small arch that was etched in 1934. These selling points just didn't ring as true to him on that day. They made his neck tingle as he passed, representatives of maintenance and worry. So much underutilized space. So much territory to patrol. A set that could never be torn down.

The mortgage was $2,800 per month.

A rustling in the kitchen. If Catharine was home, then why wasn't her car outside? A flash of long blond hair in a sunbeam spilling in from the window over the sink. Jennifer. She was pouring a packet of wheatgrass into a waterglass.

"What are you doing home?"

Battered brown boots and tight jeans. An earth-tone blouse. Long, tan arms adorned with chunky rock jewelry. A red headband. His daughter was dressing differently since she had started at New Paltz last September. Her presence was a shock. She should have been Upstate.

"Well hello to you too."

She was studying the nutritional facts on the back of the wheatgrass packet. He didn't say anything.

"I just couldn't deal with being up there today. Don't be like Mom."

When she spoke the words "up there" she had winced as if in pain.

"Is everything cool, Jennifer?"

His head felt as if it were being filled with a harsh, lacerating light. He swallowed hard, thinking about the time, around a month previous, when she had come home unexpectedly in the middle of classes and the cold, insect-like glare Catharine had fixed in her.

"For 13 grand a semester I think she can *deal*," she had said. "Does she think it was easy for me to 'deal' with Mary Ann Liebert today? Does she think it's easy for the thousands suffering from stomach cancer to 'deal' with that?"

His daughter was looking at him now, no doubt wondering what he was thinking. It saddened him to see that she appeared frightened.

"It's wonderful to see you, Jenny."

He gave her a reassuring pat on the shoulder. She pushed his hand away playfully, studying his face.

"You look spooked as hell, man," she told him.

Tofu tacos. This is the meal Jennifer had prepared for them, and it was much better than he had expected. He even went in for another after finishing the four she had placed on his plate. They hadn't said a word to one another while he loaded the dishwasher and she prepared dinner, but she hummed the entire time. He hadn't felt this relaxed in quite a long time.

She didn't eat much. He wondered if she had a hippie boyfriend up there in New Paltz, one of those kids he remembered from his own college days who plays hacky sack out on the quad for all of eternity. This would explain the new fashion choices. He wondered if her and her dorm-mate placed towels in the cracks under their door so the RAs wouldn't catch them smoking pot, much like the reverse air flow system he and his dorm-mate had used all those years ago which utilized an intricate system of standing fans that created an air pocket vacuum that swept all the smoke in the room out the window. The next year that dorm-mate had passed out drunk in a dumpster and was crushed to death in a trash compacter.

Is she going to fail out of school? And if she fails out of school, then would she be here cooking him vegetarian dinners forevermore? She was clearing their plates, placing the leftovers for Catharine by the microwave. She noticed him watching her. Her smile was as easy as always, but worry tinged her eyes.

Perhaps it wouldn't be such a bad thing if she never left. Without her the empty space sang louder. Square footage devoid of purpose, lawless zones collecting dust and chaos. The empire had expanded its borders too far and could no longer control its peripheries. This is how rot and degeneration breeds.

"Since when do you know how to cook?"

She shrugged and said, "You seem changed, Dad."

He nodded.

Catharine didn't show up until nine. She hadn't texted or called. He and Jennifer were in the middle of an episode of *Little People Meth Hoarders* in the living room. A beep from the alarm system. A jiggling of the lock. Her hair was tied back even though it had been down when she left the house that morning. She didn't say hello. Noticing Jennifer, she closed her eyes for a moment as if steeling herself. "What are *you* doing here?" She echoed his earlier question, only with much more venom than he had mustered. Jennifer began stammering. He tuned it all out, thinking of all the dusty crevices within the house beyond their reach, out of their immediate control. After a brief volley of raised voices, Catharine put up her hand to stop whatever Jennifer was saying. She noticed the television, remarked, "There's so much wrong with this show I don't even know where to begin," tucked her bag under her arm and blew through the room like a dark breeze. Whatever air there had been in the room was sucked out in her slipstream. He didn't follow her. Jennifer rolled her eyes and let out a breath. The sound of heels clicking through the hallway, up the stairs, above their heads. They turned uneasily back to the massive television.

It had been three years since he and his wife had last kissed hello.

He didn't run across Catharine again until nearly half an hour later. This run-in occurred in the kitchen. She appeared surprised to find him in there pouring a glass of water from the BRITA container. He tensed up, but there was nothing that could be done. They were in the same space now. They were going to have to interact.

"Why is the dishwasher running now?"

He didn't say anything, moving to place the container back in the fridge.

"You have *one* chore. And now there's no bowls. Thanks a lot.

He opened the cabinet, pointing out two bowls sitting on the shelf.

"That's only two."

He closed the cabinet. "There's only one of you."

Shaking her head, she moved for the cabinet. He was halfway out of the room before she asked, "Why is she skipping classes again?"

He stopped in the doorway, speaking to her with his back turned.

"She just needs to work her own way in. She's always been like that. Nobody can tell her to do anything. She needs to figure it out for herself. She always does. You know that."

"And she's dressing like Janis fucking Joplin."

"It's more Joni Mitchell, actually. Laurel Canyon style. Look, it's upstate New York. New Paltz. Even the water is crunchy up there."

"Whatever."

He turned to her. "We all just need to find our own small space, our own compartment, and make it as efficient as we can. She'll find hers once she realizes that all the rest, all this empty space, is just chaos and ruin. She's searching for it already. I can see it in her face. You would too if you could only bring yourself to look at her.

"Did something happen to you today? Are you having some sort of lame religious conversion? That would be *just* what we need."

They had stopped asking one another how their days went long ago.

"Anyway the electric is due. Someone ran the central *a lot* this summer and I know it wasn't me."

He pointed toward the ceiling. "It's all this unused space. It's a lot to heat and cool. And it doesn't do anybody one bit of good. It isn't utilized in any way. It just sits on us and crushes us slowly into debt."

She was pouring a box of Grape-Nuts into the bowl, wincing with each word he said, each breath he breathed.

"Well, perhaps there would be less debt if you hadn't been in the exact same position, at the exact same salary, for over five years."

"I'm talking about psychic debt, Catharine. Psychic debt."

She eyed him with a fierce interest, seemingly unaware that the cereal was now spilling onto the counter. He continued.

"Money begets holes, and those holes eat the money, so then you have make more, which only begets more holes. There's really no way to win against that cycle unless you quit the game entirely."

"Beget this."

She let the bowl drop into the sink. He was amazed it didn't shatter. She moved to leave the room but he stood in her way.

"Don't you want to downsize? Don't you realize that all this…" He swept his arm to display the high ceilings"…is bearing down on us in a damaging way? Now that Jennifer is out of the house…"

"It doesn't look like she's out of the house to me. As a matter of fact, it doesn't look like she's going anywhere. It reminds me of someone else I know well. Now move, please."

He stood his ground, but he could feel his resolve slipping.

"I really don't want to do this right now."

He pitied her in that moment. Standing with her eyes closed. Her feet bare. Laundry-shrunk pajama pants barely covering her calves. She rarely appeared this vulnerable.

"I'm exhausted. You're talking crazy riddles tonight. It makes my head spin. Now would you please, please, *please move*."

He nodded but didn't budge.

"Can't we just go back to our cold war," she pleaded through clenched teeth.

From the living room, the volume on the TV went up. The *Little People Meth Hoarders* closing credits, a rap song with jittery keyboard lines and distorted base. They had been speaking in hushed tones so that Jennifer wouldn't hear them.

"If you don't move now I'm going to go over there and get a knife, and I'm not sure if it's you or me who's going to get it. Either way I can guarantee I won't be hearing your metaphysical fucking nonsense anymore."

He stepped aside.

By midnight he was sitting alone watching a show that tracked the lives of a group of 20-something girls in Brooklyn who had bad luck with dating. Jennifer had fallen asleep for an hour on the opposite end of the couch, woke up yawning, then headed off for her bedroom. He didn't tell her that Catharine already had that room targeted as a home office. Before exiting she had patted him on the head and, pulling a pin from her jeans, had presented it to him. The pin said *Deserters*. He swore he smelled weed on her clothing.

He missed weed.

From the hallway he could see the door to the room he and Catharine used to share. It was open a crack, with the glow from an iPad emanating from within. He could picture her sullen face aglow in the digital light, scanning, scanning, scanning. In that moment he was glad he no longer had to lie next to her.

In the basement his sleeping kit was stashed behind the pullout couch he had been sleeping on for the past two years. In order to fall asleep most nights, he would envision a press conference in his mind where reporters would shout questions at him as he sat at a long table in front of a single microphone, just inane questions about the smallest details of the day that had just passed. "Are you going to finish the spreadsheet on Montana Smart Sani-Saver customer analytics by the due date, sir?" This press conference worked to compress his thoughts. It was a debriefing process, and he would usually be asleep by the third or fourth question. This wasn't the case that night. The presser went on and on until the reporters had run out of questions. It must have been the small hours of the morning by the time he finally drifted off.

The dream was so vivid it shook him into consciousness. It wasn't yet dawn. He had been alone in a vast expanse. It was neither day nor night. There were no distinguishing characteristics to the landscape. It wasn't outer space, nor was it Earth. An endless blank. Millions of miles of unoccupied space. Unutilized. Wasted. The weight and chaos of the expanse weighed on him heavily. It made him sad. But in the dream he was planning something. The specifics were vague, but the end goal was to break down the space. To compartmentalize the miles. To put them to use. Not one wasted inch. In the dream he had it all figured out. He knew this was the last time he would gaze upon the terrifying dimensions. Implementation was imminent.

A solution for desolation.

Pains wracked his ribcage and his eyeballs felt dry and sandy in their sockets. He sat up in the subterranean darkness. 2200 square feet in the house above him. At least 2000 of those square feet unused and out of his control. What was that solution? What were the specifics of the plan? He had awakened before it was carried out. Now he might never know.

He stayed still, not wanting the peripheral debris of the dream to fall away. He had been so sure. He had known exactly what to do. But he couldn't get it back. The knowledge had slipped away with his awakening.

It was just when he had given up, when he resigned himself to his doom within the empire of wasted space, that it came to him. He had fallen into an uneasy sleep when there was a jab to his synapses, a laser point of light so sharp it made him sit upright in pain. Just three small white font letters:

pod

On the morning train he was thinking about the electric bill. Every seat in the compartment was taken. He stood by the doors, leaning against the wall under a sign that said, "No Alcoholic Beverages. No Spitting. No hoverboards." Several others stood with him, one reading a paper and the other two scowling at their phones, scanning, scanning, scanning. He just stared straight ahead. The only information Catharine had given him was that the bill was due. She hadn't stated how much it was. She hadn't volunteered a payment arrangement. Was he paying? Were they going half on it?

The trivial mechanics involved in maintaining a dead empire.

He felt protein deprived and weak, even though he had consumed the tofu taco meal the night before plus three hard-boiled eggs and toast that morning. His head felt shrunken and caved. He had spent the pre-dawn hours in the basement in the dark, scrolling so hard on his phone that the tip of his pointer finger still ached.

He was researching the pods.

There were four locations throughout the city. 39th Street. 51st Street. Times Square. Williamsburg. He couldn't find the exact stats on how many pods were available in each location, but by his estimate there would have to be over a thousand pods in total. It had started with one location, but the popularity was so massive that there were now four. Rumors of new pods throughout the city were alive and well on various real estate blogs and forums. A pod hotel had opened up in Washington D.C. as well.

The pods were spreading.

The types of pods available differed in each location, but the premise was simple. For as little as $65 per night one could enjoy a clean and efficient "single pod" with a small, comfortable-looking bed, a desk, a flatscreen television mounted to the wall, a place to hang clothes, a safe, and a similarly small but well-designed bathroom encased in glass and featuring a rainfall showerhead. Efficiency in its least diluted form. There were also bunk pods which could fit entire families, but it was the single pods which most interested him. These were the pods which seemed to hold the answer.

$65 per night. This would be less that $500 per week. At $2,000 per month this would be far less than most individuals paid for an apartment in the city. It would be significantly cheaper than his current mortgage. A crafty, upwardly mobile but temporarily cash strapped individual, for example somebody who has just obtained gainful employment but has yet to build up the cash reserve needed for first month and security deposit on an apartment, could ease into the pod life for as long as needed. Switch up pod locations each week. Stay off the radar.

High-end transience.

And then there were the pods themselves, space age and coffin sized, all the makings of an uncomplicated, efficient existence. Only the basic amenities needed for comfort, not a single excess, nothing weighing you down, no physical or psychic clutter, no wasted space, every single inch utilized for maximum efficiency. This was a completely compartmentalized existence, sleek and trim, safe in the maelstrom.

As the sun finally began spilling through the thin-slat basement windows, he had been deep in research on the history of the pod concept. The main inspiration seemed to be the "capsule hotels" which had been popping up in Japan since the late '70s and spreading across Asia over the mass-population decades. These looked incredibly appealing to him, just tiny capsules with a mattress where one could sleep in a highly efficient darkness. The perfect solution for dense urban territories, the compartmentalization of chaos. The concept of the "house" or the "apartment" had been slipping in Asia for years. The thirst for space had been quenched. The final volley had been launched in the war on clutter, and all it took was a designated capsule for a productive citizen to lay their head at night. They could keep moving, keep working, throw off the Beast's square foot shackles, the mortgage payments and the nine broken mountain bikes taunting them from the garage.

These capsule hotels were originally treated as a mere curiosity in the Western press even as "luxury" capsule establishments were birthed from Singapore to St. Petersburg. How odd that these funny little Japanese businessmen would stuff themselves into their funny little capsules at night! Let us all smirk at the Capsule People from our palatial suburban vinyl-sided empires with their 2.5 bathrooms, 1.5 of which remained unused but still required cleaning and upgrades.

And yet here they were popping up on the East Coast in the form of pod hotels. Four and counting and massively popular. It was only logical that they would start in New York City, the closest beast to your typical Blade Runner Asian cityscape. Their success and expansion within the Boroughs could only mean plans for pods within other US urban areas. In recent articles he sensed a loosening of judgment, a creeping acceptance in the face of coastal overpopulation and the erasing of the middle class. A viable, efficient phoenix was rising.

Through the train door window he watched as the scenery faded from suburban confusion to the condensed, logical grids of Upper Manhattan. He felt a great sugar rush of relief that made his mouth water.

The age of the pods had arrived.

The 8th floor of a boxy office complex on 3rd Avenue. He had spent the entire morning in his office. Not once did he venture to the break room or bathrooms. It wasn't actually "his" office since he shared it with his colleague Janize, but she worked from her home in Connecticut three-days-per-week. He had been staring out the window at the roof of a six-floor walkup where an elaborate movie set had been staged. There were floodlights even though it was broad day, and a scattering of prop debris had been added to make the roof's surface appear even scuzzier than it already had been, upturned and dented trash cans, false surfaces covered in forced graffiti. He watched as several lackeys walked across the black tar surface liberally sprinkling trash from canvas bags. There were a number of trailers set up on the roof plus a long table that served as a food and coffee station. He wondered how they had gotten the trailers up there.

All of these buildings…offices and condominiums and apartments, built from the ground to the sky. But still it wasn't high enough for him. There was still too much non-utilized square footage, too much chaos. Imagine the space that could be saved if they were to build it all higher, up into the fly zones, if they were to condense the spaces down to pods, down to the bare essentials, every person entitled to their individual compartment, all equal, all free.

Not much was happening on the email front. Many of the higher-ups took long vacations in the summers, prolonging their marriages, alleviating the pressures of their individual empires through temporary displacement. His own boss, who was located in the Dutch office, was one of them. There was one report that needed to be done, compiling the analytics of Montana Smart Sani-Saver customers, but that wasn't due until the 30th. Smart Sani-Saver was a brand of sanitary covers for smartphones, fully armed with a cache of truly alarming stats on germ infestation rates for these devices. Started by a Dutch couple around the time of the invention of the iPhone, Smart Sani-Saver had coasted on the cresting, paranoiac waves of germaphobia, eventually expanding to four offices world-wide. Amsterdam. London. New York. Los Angeles. He had been with Smart Sani-Saver for 9 years, working his way from Analytics Associate to Senior Analytics Associate. He really had no idea how customer analytics had become his career. His degree had been in Marketing with a minor in French Litera-ture. This slow motion career development had been a source of great personal bewilderment over the years, but he did not hate his job, and this was more than could be said for 90% of the people he knew.

Through the half-open office door the floor was empty and hushed. The low end abrasion of clacking keyboards. The occasional bent soul scampering past on their way to the bank of printers or back to their high-walled cubicle. Perfect hiding places. He was thinking about how efficient it would be if all of those workers were to live in their cubicles as well. Maximum efficiency. Utilized space. He shook his head as if to clear it. Intrusive thoughts. What in the hell was happening to him? Steeling himself, he rose from his chair and set off in the direc-tion of the Keurig machines.

In the break room stood two golden beings. He had never seen them before. The boy had a swept-over shag cut of the finest child-like locks and a hopelessly wrinkled white dress shirt. The girl was lithe and tanned with hair the color of honey spilling to the small of her back. Glowing, healthy skin stretched taut across their faces, clashing cruelly with the chipped paint ambiance of the office break room. The two of them stopped speaking as he entered. The blond fixed her shagged companion with a benevolent smile. He moved for the coffee makers, feeling their eyes on him the entire way.

"We are Deserters, my friend. Both of us."

It took him a long moment to process that he was being spoken to. Looking up, he was confronted with two searching, wide-open smiles and four shiny, well-moisturized cheeks. Cherubs.

"Pardon?"

It was the first time that day he had heard his own voice.

"Deserters, sir. That last necessary step. We were just discussing precipice points."

The blond girl said this.

"Um...*precipice points?*"

She shot him a sly look, as if he was playing some type of game with her and she was delighted by it. Her friend spoke.

"Have you yet to reach your precipice?"

This was definitely a set up. He scanned the room for co-conspirators filming the scene on their phones.

Then it hit him.

The pin. *Deserters.* Jennifer had given it to him the night before. In a sleep-deprived state of abandon that morning he had pinned it to the side of his dress shirt.

"I thought 'Deserters' was a band or something."

His coffee was done. This was just another failed conversation, another missed connection. But their smiles had only expanded, stretching out the pair's soft, almost translucent lips. Their eyes gleamed as if he had just said something revelatory or witty. Nobody had ever gazed upon him with such acceptance. Most people in New York stood with their arms crossed in an "X" formation even when speaking to their spouses or close friends. Full-on defense. This pair let their limbs hang loose, exposed to harm. They had *faith*.

"Your precipice is soon to come," the boy said.

Which Smart Sani-Saver department did these translucent twin beings emerge from? His first thought was Finance. Nobody ever saw anyone from that department, which would explain why he had never run across them previously. Studying their faces, however, he realized they were far too open and bright for that darkest of worlds. Sales perhaps? Why yes, it would have to be, for at that moment he would have gladly purchased anything they had to offer.

"What's your name?"

It occurred to him that they may be from some deep internal investigations unit at the company. A honey trap.

"Why do you want to know my name?"

"So that we can invite you."

The girl said this as if it were obvious, like he was being coy.

"We really have to get going. But before we do we would really like your..."

He stated his name as if he were at roll call, even though he hadn't wanted to. They had willed him to state it, cast some sort of soft spell. They nodded their thanks. They appeared relieved, thrilled even. Apparently this bit of insignificant information was all they had wanted from him, since immediately upon his stating it they turned to go. The girl gave him a wave as she followed her friend out of the break room. He stood with his cup of coffee burning his palm.

What had he just done?

Back in his office, his designated work station. His heart raced. The filming on the roof was wrapping for the day. Men in headsets ran around pulling down the boom mics. 3:00. Film crews worked short hours, apparently. He hadn't asked for their names, those two units of light from the break room. It just hadn't seemed important at the time. Their mere presence was so refreshingly alien that nothing else meant anything at all. But now he regretted it. Without their names he couldn't track them down in the Smart Sani-Saver directory. It worried him greatly that it would be the last time he'd ever see them. Never again would he be cast into the thrilling head rush of their certainty and acceptance.

Deserters.

Precipice points.

He clicked save on the Montana customer analytics spreadsheet. After a long while his screen went dark.

Six o'clock and still staring at the now empty movie set. The trash they had scattered was blowing off the rooftop in a light wind. For a long time he had been standing by the window, shuffling in order to stretch his sore legs. Watching the cityscape with singular focus, the intrusive thoughts returned. Close it all in. Confine the quarters. Eliminate the expanse.

A text popped up from Jennifer. Hours earlier he had sent her a missive. *Deserters?* He twirled the pin between his fingers. But her reply supplied no clues.

Dad can I talk to you about something? No Mom.

Perhaps she was being expelled for poor grades or a series of disciplinary infractions. He wondered if she was on her way to jail. Regardless he was pleased that she texted him. At one point the text conversations with Catharine stretched the entire day, so many per month that the bills would be massive. It had been at least three years since the last time she had sent him a day text.

The stark silence of an after-hours office. He had no idea what he was still doing there, but he didn't wish to leave. Thoughts of the 6:21 train horrified him, the transition from the rigid city grids to the horrifying space of the suburbs. Sensing a presence, he turned to find a woman in a blue outfit standing in his office doorway. She was wielding an intricate cleaning device with multiple automated dusters and a contracting handle.

Something in her surprised, feral stare made him realize there truly was no shelter.

Back on the street. Third Avenue. He found himself pulled toward 39th Street as if by a light but insistent magnetic force. He didn't have much time, not a minute to spare to stop and stare. But there it was, the pod hotel, a pre-war building gutted and stuffed with small, efficient units. Not a drop of wasted space, a minimal chaos level. All of the buildings should be utilized as such. Condense the spatial impulse, isolationism through strategic crowding. Round up the masses and stack them to the sky.

On the street outside the Grand Central side entrance a man had fashioned a comfortable-looking home utilizing two massive Amazon Prime boxes. He paused to stare longingly at the setup until someone behind him gave a short, sharp shove to his back. Inside the station he marveled at the lines that had formed in front of the ticket windows and machines. People standing single file with only inches in between, staring at their phones or taking hesitant sips from gleaming, green matcha lattes, cold to their immediate neighbors but warmed by the crush of their bodies.

The last thing he wants is to get on the train. But where else would he go? Each weekday he toiled eight-plus hours within the city limits but had no real connection to its inner workings, its grids and compartments, its dark bars and bright Apple stores, it's lush secrets. The commuters behind him on the platform were getting pissed at his dawdling. Pointed sighs and stifled curses, mass transit rage. He felt lightheaded, hollow. Thinking of Jennifer, he forced himself to take the tough first step onto the train compartment stairs.

Just another draining threshold.

It had saddened him on the previous day, but on that day's commute the sight of the receding urban scenery instilled within him a sense of desperation that was nearly overwhelming. He felt seriously weighted down. Condensed street grids gave way to vast empty swaths. He stared on in horror. A brutal car crash it was difficult to turn away from. When the developments and high school football fields took over he could stand it no longer. Moving for the back of the car, fumbling with the sliding lock on the bathroom door, his fingers shaking so hard they could no longer grip. Looking at his face full-on in the unflattering light of the small, scuffed mirror above the sink.

He was amazed to find he was crying.

This time there really was nobody home. No Jennifer ambushes. He took off his shoes and paced the house, appraising the poison clutter, the terrifying square feet. Just the thought of the backyard beyond the darkening windows was enough to make the back of his throat vibrate with fear, an emperor awakened from a placid dream into a self-created nightmare world.

The vastness was far too great to be responsible for.

By eight he was seated on a stool in the kitchen with his eyes clamped shut. It wasn't meditation, nor was it an attempt to hide. He simply didn't want to witness the space between himself and the high ceilings or feel the long arms of the hallways. Two beeps from the front door alarm, steps in the living room. It was immediately clear that these footfalls didn't belong to Catharine. They didn't ring with the singular, stalking confidence he had heard thousands of times through the floorboards of the house. A half-formed stride. Jennifer.

His eyes were open by the time she reached the kitchen.

"Where have you been?"

She shrugged, moving for the fridge.

"I was thinking maybe you'd gone back to school."

She stared into the fridge for a moment, drumming her fingers against the door. With a sigh, she closed it without retrieving anything.

"About your text…"

"Look, can we just have a smoke out back and talk?"

An insane invitation. So alien it took several long moments to register. Jennifer smoked? And if so, then why wouldn't she keep this hidden?

"You smoke cigarettes?"

A sudden sharp exhale. Jennifer never did learn how to laugh.

"*Cigarettes?* Vape, you idiot."

He didn't really even know what that was.

"That sounds lovely."

Apple Whirlwind. The concept sounded awful, but it went down incredibly smooth. Nearly an hour later they were on the patio with their feet propped up on deck chairs. Fruity vape mist clouded the air. They had barely spoken a word.

"You said you needed to talk to me about something."

She nodded, exhaling a ghostly plume.

"Lots of students don't do well their first year. It's an adjustment."

"Classes are easy," she assured him.

"Ok."

He itched to get back inside, away from the dark expanse of the backyard. It had once seemed small to him, pithy, a drastic sign of failure when compared to the intricate acreage accompanying the houses several blocks to the west. It now felt like a cumbersome albatross, a neglected jungle at the far end of a vast estate breeding hostile natives and poison serpents. One night they would overtake the main house.

"School itself will be fine. I've just run into a small issue. I'm hoping it will blow over but really I'm not so sure."

He placed his head in his hands. This moment had finally come.

"Pregnancies generally don't just blow over…"

That exhale again. She slapped him on the shoulder while handing him the space age smoking apparatus.

"I'm not fucking pregnant."

His head shot back up as if on an automated spring.

"I'm sorry," she said. I know I said I wanted to talk about it. And I do. Maybe just not right now. I'm tired. And I'm enjoying this moment with you."

He nodded. He couldn't recall the last time they had hung out without some sort of purpose attached to it.

"What was *your* first year of college like?"

He exhaled an impressive plume, coughing only a little.

"The roommate I was paired with my first semester. The first weekend he went out and got too wasted. At some point he fell and cut his ear. Just a small gash. But his blood was so thin from the drinking. I came back to the dorm to find him passed out in the middle of the room. Drenched in blood. I thought he'd been stabbed."

"Oh god."

"There weren't cell phones then. I had to go to the front desk to have the ambulance called. The RAs were so stoned they couldn't figure out how to dial out. It took a long time. When the ambulance and cops showed up, they thought he'd been assaulted. I was held as a suspect for a couple hours. Handcuffed in the back of a cop car."

"Wait, what?"

"It wasn't until later, at the hospital, when they realized it was just a minor cut to his ear. He had alcohol poisoning though. Was legally dead for almost a minute. I forget his name. His parents came and took him away."

She was smiling.

"So you mean to tell me you were actually a murder suspect?"

"For a couple of hours, yes."

She nodded at this thoughtfully, tilting her head slightly to the left.

"I've never thought of you as a human being before this moment," she said.

The thought of those dorms had comforted him. He hated them at the time, but now they struck him as a model of efficient living.

"About that pin you gave me last night…"

They hadn't heard the patio door slide open.

"Why is the dishwasher not loaded?"

He didn't turn to face Catharine, but her presence made the back of his neck burn cold. "I did it yesterday,"

"What are you two doing?" She cut him off, getting to the real question she had wanted to ask from the start.

He held up the vape device for her to observe.

"Interesting."

Jennifer appeared frightened, sensing the incoming question before it hit.

"You haven't returned to school yet?"

"Next week, Mom. Soon."

Catharine nodded. "Have you even had dinner?"

They shook their heads.

"Well, my show is on." Jennifer moved past her mother and into the house. He admired her lack of fear when passing by her. He remained in the chair, open to attack.

"She may be in college, but you're not."

He didn't say anything or even look at her. It took him a moment to realize she had extended her hand to him.

"Are you going to let me hit that or what?"

Passing her the device, they exchanged the first conspiratorial smirk they had shared in many years.

It always seemed to happen in the kitchen, the volleys and strikes, the arms folded in defensive poses, flash floods from long-ago rains. The kitchen was where the beasts were trotted out to play.

"Forgive me if I resort to minor irresponsibility in order to connect with my own daughter," he was saying. The venom behind his words surprised him. "I miss her around here."

It was true that Jennifer's absence during her first semester at New Paltz had been a disaster for their domestic relations. She had long acted as the ideal buffer. Without her the cold war was threatening to heat up.

"One shouldn't even be thinking of such things."

There they were, the folded arms protecting her core, two sentries that would never welcome him again. "Wake up to the new world," she was saying. "People are on their own to progress as far as they can in life."

"That's a *cold* worldview."

"It's a *practical* worldview. It's *reality*. It's what keeps the machinery functioning. Life transitions are key for the progress of everything. One transitions on to college, out of the house, not eating up the household food and wasting the cash spent sending them to school in the first place, all those dorm fees and meal plans, working their way toward building their own household. This leaves the original empire to flourish. It's progress. It's the way things work. A drain on the household can be fatal."

Talk of households made him feel all the wasted square feet within their empire come crashing upon his shoulders in light spasms.

"If we could just downgrade this particular...um...*household* to a less cumbersome setup..."

"Are you still on this? You're talking like it's your first time on acid."

"...then some more compassion could be brought into the picture. There would be less of a household to drain. More forgiveness could be factored in, more slack. What if she has a real problem, Catharine? What if it goes beyond your average late teenage ennui?"

She winced visibly at the word "ennui".

"She's an adult now and will need to deal with it. If we allow her to fade back in here each time she has some sort of minor issue, one day she'll be 44 and moving back in because her 2nd husband didn't load the dishwasher and was caught smoking with their delinquent daughter on the back porch."

At which point had she become so cold? At what exact moment had the two of them sunk into such an impersonal business partnership? Like with all slow progressions, a definitive precipice point, as the two beings in the break room had been discussing, could never be pinpointed. It's like when one domestic partner loses or gains a significant amount of weight. Can their partner look back and pinpoint a specific day or week when that weight came into play? It's a glacial progression, bleeding in over expansive periods of time. One day they wake up and realize the person sleeping next to them bears no resemblance to the one they linked up with all those years ago.

But this was far worse. The change wasn't physical. A connection had been snuffed out, two beings forced to do lone maintenance work for their unwieldy and confusing empire, staying out of one another's way as much as possible. On one night fifteen years previous he had walked with her after a party, for blocks and blocks in the wee hours. Even in the harsh, pre-LED streetlights her hair gleamed like a protective halo, her skin tone translucent but the skin stretched firm over intriguing bursts of bone. It gave him such a rush to observe her, to consider that there could be more nights like this stretching on infinitely, a metallic tang on the roof of his mouth, teeth tingling, his synapses so alive it felt as if they were short circuiting one-by-one with loud pops. And here she was standing in the middle of a large, gleaming kitchen many years and many strife-struck moons later, fixing him with a murderous stare somewhere close to pure hate.

The difference was stunning.

His knees gave way and he sank down onto the floor.

"Oh god what's wrong with you?"

Looking to the ceiling. He could have stacked her on his shoulders and she still wouldn't be able to touch it. A withering realization.

"Why do we even need this?"

He knocked his head twice against the dishwasher.

"We have *hands*. We can *do dishes*. We always did before. And look at the size of this kitchen? What's it all for? I'm being yelled at for sitting on a patio that's never used. A downstairs bathroom rotting away. Never used. Closets jammed with relics. A garage jammed with derelict refuse…"

She eyed him like a homeless man acting up on the subway, a combination of self-reflexive defense and fake pity.

"What. Do. You. Want. Then." She clapped her hands on each word.

He didn't immediately respond. She stamped her foot in frustration.

"Let's downgrade, Catharine. Let's ditch the relics, the poison space. Let's enclose ourselves, put fficiency first. I don't know, we could move to the city?"

A smirk from Catharine. She had known this question was going to come. Her answer was perfectly executed as if rehearsed, simply counting off her reasons as if reading them from a long list like a menu at a restaurant.

"I work here. I like it here. We still owe 380K on this house. We worked our whole lives for this house, this 'poison space' and all these 'relics'. Fought our *whole lives*. It isn't poison to me. It's comfort. I'm claustrophobic for chrissakes."

He tried to think if he ever knew she was claustrophobic. Had he forgotten or had he truly never known? Perhaps he hadn't noticed. This possibility made him sad.

"We can barely coexist in 3800 square feet. How would we hold up in a 500 square foot one bedroom apartment? Plus, if you think that newly far-out daughter of ours will be transitioning out of here anytime soon, then keep in mind she's skulking around her room up there right now just like when she was 15."

He had been fully prepared for these counterpoints, but the truth in them was so great they hit him like a deftly executed round of punches.

"I don't know." His confidence was slipping. " It's just that we put everything into this white wooden box, this flimsy empire, but all the space and clutter just *eats and eats and eats* away at it. It's constantly under attack. The reserves are depleted. The armies are tired and tattered, Catharine. *It's all going to fall.* Unless we get out from under it, unless we pull away. Let the jungle take it back. Let the rebel factions absorb it. Don't you see? It's a war we no longer have to fight."

Her arms remained crossed, but she wasn't trying to interject. Was he chipping away at her exoskeletal exterior? His own voice rang in his ears with great pain, and he wondered if it just might be getting through.

"If we lost the space, then maybe we could try sleeping in the same bed again. We could even go back to binge watching *Shameless.* Maybe it's the space that has killed..." He gestured frantically at the air between them, "...this."

A brief burst of light, the flash of the wicked mischief smirk he had once known, lit up her face. She exhaled hard through gritted teeth, obviously relishing what she was about to say.

"Have fun in the basement tonight."

She turned and walked from the kitchen, leaving him crouched on the floor.

"Ok just walk away," he called after her. "I'm not trying to fight here, Catharine. It's not a confrontation. I'm trying to pull you in with me on a *conspiracy.*"

Her steps rattled the hallway floorboards. He thought of the time shortly after they had first moved in together when her friend Tanya was over and they had smoked some of her pot, which may or may not have been laced with angel dust. For hours after Tanya left they had sat cross-legged on the bed staring into one another's eyes. This trance went on until well after daybreak, and at some point the whites of her eyes swallowed his entire vision. Neither of them spoke a word until the drug started wearing off and her shape came back into focus and the void receded. This night had come up often in those first years they were together, and they both agreed they may have gone insane or plummeted out the apartment windows had they not been there to stabilize one another. This night hadn't been mentioned in a good number of years by that point. It didn't seem like it had ever really happened. Deadened by the decades. It would most likely never be brought up again.

She was gone. No response. Most likely she hadn't even heard him.

A ghost in peril.

Again he couldn't sleep. Again the sheer weight of those oppressive square feet sat heavy on his chest. It must have been around midnight when he ascended the stairs. He wasn't thirsty and had no need to use the bathroom. Standing in the after-hours kitchen he noticed a blue light glowing on the patio, the end of an electronic smoking device. Jennifer. She appeared happy to see him. They were outriders on the periphery of the kingdom. Sobered by marital roadblocks, he couldn't even manage a smile back.

"I couldn't sleep and didn't want to wake up Catharine so..."

Jennifer laughed, shaking her head adoringly.

"I know you sleep in the basement, Dad. The charade is over."

He nodded, impressed.

"Certain arrangements are needed in order to maintain empirical functions."

She nodded thoughtfully.

"Is this why you guys want me out of the house so badly? So you can have my room? So you can sleep without fearing spider attacks?"

"We just want for you to be able to transition into the outer realm."

He sneered in distaste at his use of Catharine's terminology. She passed him the pen, a different one than earlier. He inhaled. This vape had very little flavor and seared the back of his throat slightly.

"What's been going on with you, dude? The vibes are way strange around here. Even stranger than when I left."

He passed her the pen. He couldn't think of any words. A minor haze was slowly whitewashing his mind.

"Are you trying to sabotage all this? Are you losing your footing or something? Like the dad in *Igby Goes Down*?"

"I've, well, I've been thinking a lot about space and..."

"Space?"

"Not, like, outer...and not inner...but this..." He swept his arm over the dark side of the house, the small sweep of the yard.

Again she nodded. He waved the pen away. He did not like this particular vape.

"I've been thinking about space as well. Like how fucking small my dorm room is. If my roommie brings her boyfriend over, it's as if *I'm* having sex with him. That's how close our beds are."

Now it was his turn to nod incomprehensibly.

He refused the pen a second time. Something told him this device wasn't fully legal. It had been a long time since he was last properly stoned. Every sound, from their voices to the clink of the glass Jennifer laid on the patio table, seemed

36

double-amplified. He expected lights in the neighboring houses to switch on one-by-one. He expected Catharine to make a hostile walk-on at any moment.

"Here's the deal," Jennifer started, then paused.

Her words rang out like a shrill riot in his skull. He beckoned for her to continue.

"I'll spare you the finer details. Give it to you straight. Are you ready for it? Because I'm only serving this up once."

He wasn't so sure he was ready for it, but she began. Each rapid-fire point was emphasized with a punch to the air from her right fist.

"My roommie. Samantha. The one with the loud bed habits? We went in on a deal. Nothing big. A little pot. A little acid. Personal use. Sam's friend went in as well. Chlorinde. She knew the dealer. His name is Wheel. Used to be a student. Dropped out. Sells shit out of Kingston. Dude went *total townie.*"

Each point hit him hard. Drugs. Misspent cash. College brats turned townie dealers. Kingston. He envisioned a soot-stained bungalow with tie-dyed sheets over the windows.

"Wheel fronted the stuff. We're just pretty enough, I guess. Then Chlorinde, oh god that Chlorinde, some say she got pregnant. Others say her parents had her locked up. Suicide attempt. Whatever. She blew town. Dropped out. Nobody's heard from her. She took the whole stash, and she never came up with her share."

"Is this Wheel character looking for you?"

"Wheel doesn't come around New Paltz much anymore. Some say he's wanted. Others say it's some local beef with a different crew."

"I can't believe you're talking about beefs and drug crews. Just a year ago you'd never seen a homeless person."

"Just small town drug game nonsense," she assured him. "But he's put out word at Moon Light and Karma Road. He's a townie now so he knows all the servers. He's gone fully native."

"What *word* did Wheel put out, Jennifer? What does this even mean? Word about *what*?"

At this she paused. The glazed, tingling feeling from the vape hit had taken a hard turn. His chest felt tight. He leaned forward, hugging himself.

"Well, Chlorinde was in Moon two weeks ago and the barista guy with three teeth passed a note along with her matcha latte. "Karma's a bitch, and so are you, the Wheel is turnin', and it's comin' for you."

"He's threatening you with Journey lyrics?"

"Grateful Dead, actually. This is Upstate New York."

"This explains the difficult transition."

"Transition?"

"Transition to the outer-world, Jennifer."

She nodded. "You really do want my bedroom, don't you?"

He waved away this suggestion. He wanted none of it.

"I was transitioning just fine, thank you very much." She extended her arm and twirled her fingers as if expecting a round of applause. "That is, until The Wheel rolled onto the scene."

Something occurred to him.

"So you were the *responsible* one in this drug deal?"

"That is such a YOU thing to ask."

She gave him a pronounced sidelong glance.

"Just please don't tell me you're proud of me."

She rose to her feet, yawning. He was grinning in the dark. She patted him twice on the head. Before sliding the patio door shut, she said, "I found that pin for a dollar in a junk shop. No idea what it means. I thought it was a band or something."

Back in the basement. Watching an actual DVD since the WiFi was choppy underground. *Withnail & I.* The final scene where Withnail stands in a park in the pouring rain and recites Shakespeare to a dog. This was a scene that had once made him weep uncontrollably for five solid minutes. It had been at least ten years since that viewing, and it disturbed him greatly to find he could no longer relate. Punching the power button, he let the room sink into darkness. All that clutter, covering him over like an acidic film, coating his lungs, drying out his eyes. He didn't want to see it any longer, yet each and every relic taking up that basement hellscape called to him in the dark:

A 2007 Fender Telecaster missing two strings

Two Orange tube amplifiers, one with a blown speaker

An assortment of standing lamps in various styles and colors

Three rolled up rugs from since-discarded empirical interior concepts

Two old desktop computers, one an Apple and the other a Macintosh

A rolled up tent that he knew had holes in it

Three sleeping bags, two blue and one pink

Two boxes stuffed with books, one college texts and the other mass market paperbacks

One box stuffed with CDs from the '90s

Three metal filing cabinets, two of them morphed under the weight of their contents, old bills and mortgage statements and tax documents. The Devil's paperwork

Two coffee makers, one at least a decade old

Three tubs containing mementos from Catharine's youth, one containing dolls, one containing yearbooks and diaries, and the other miscellaneous

A punching bag lying on its side

Some sort of kickboxing bag

An assortment of yoga mats in various earth tones

An exercise bike

Three skis, one snowboard

Three old non-digital cameras from the two month period five years previous when Catharine thought she was a photographer

Test tubes and tubs for the making of soap, which he had once thought would be simple

A number of mismatched chairs stacked on top of one another, designated to be brought out when "company was over"

At least three ottomans from the stressed period where they couldn't find the right design theme for the living room

A supremely ugly patchwork rocking chair which had once belonged to his long-dead grandmother

An African tribal wooden head with an elongated skull. He had no idea where it came from.

He felt a panic attack coming on like a ripple of thunder before a summer storm. A burnt sensation tinged the rims of his nostrils. He lay on his back in the subterranean dark.

The smell of damp and mold.

"Basement sealed and waterproof guaranteed."

He had been watching the pods. There were nearly always vacancies. On that morning it fascinated him that ten new pods were available in the Williamsburg location. Who were the people who had checked out? And who were the 3 individuals who had already snatched up the vacancies left in their slipstream? Budget tourists? People in the city on business? Thin souls on the fringe staying one step ahead of the winds that would eventually eviscerate them?

There were four pods available at the 39th street location and 13 up for grabs on 51st. This meant that well over a thousand pods were occupied at that very moment. These numbers were impressive to him. A transient army, a tribe of the winds, condensed and powerful just like the Metro North train he was riding on with everyone tucked neatly into their designated areas with their coffees and iPads and wheatgrass drinks, the occasional newspaper or book. The city was coming into view. The relief he felt at the sight of the outer edges of the Bronx warmed him to his core.

Moving down 3rd Avenue heading for the Smart Sani-Saver New York office, descending onto a shaky grid, off to his doom but walking on air.

"Say brotherman, can you point the way to Babylon?"

"That way." He guided the wild-eyed old man east.

The man bowed to him, his eyes glazed and his dirty robe touching the sidewalk.

He moved on humming to himself, delighted at the sight of the pedestrians on the sidewalk all lined up and walking single file as they should be.

This peace of mind held true deep into his workday. He had the office to himself once again. Much of the morning was spent disposing of some small points of clutter, a stack of sticky notes containing pen scrawls that may as well have been Sanskrit, a dead succulent he had been attempting to revive with no success, a stack of Smart Sani-Saver pens from a trade show rubber banded together. He kept one.

He liked his office, just cramped enough to breathe. Working on the Montana customer data report, columns stacked with numbers, intricate color codes, automated formulas. The end of the report was firmly in sight. Just through the office wall there were dozens of employees tucked neatly into their workspaces. Producing, producing, producing.

Everything in its right place.

The filming on the rooftop across the street was back on. Short train tracks had been set up across the roof's surface. Cameramen coasted on dollies. It looked like fun. It was then that he noticed a new email in his Outlook inbox.

There was no subject line. The email itself came from within the company. He knew this because of the Smart Sani-Saver address, but the sender's name was just an impenetrable string of letters and numbers and special figures. Was it special code? A riddle? Some sort of virus? Turning back to the sheet, he couldn't concentrate. The email, bold and unopened, stared at him from the other monitor, burning the side of his face. After several unsuccessful attempts to get back into the columns, he clicked back over and attempted to delete it but it wouldn't disappear. He tried to manually drag it into the trash folder, but again it popped right back.

Shaking his head, he closed Outlook altogether.

At some point after lunch he felt the need for a decaf. Walking past the break room entrance he took a scouting glance inside. There were no signs of the benevolent, glowing beings he had encountered the day previous. It was tough to imagine they had even been standing in that spot on the scuffed, chipped tile under the harsh break room fluorescents. Operating the Keurig machine, he overheard a conversation happening at one of the tables between two Smart Sani-Saver employees, where one of them stated:

"I was always dead set against moving so far out in Queens, but I gotta' tell ya' I appreciate the extra space."

He shook his head. Enjoy it while you can, he thought. At some point all that space is going to weigh you down.

Later on, as he sat in a bathroom stall, a rare day text chimed in from Catharine. Just a minor trifle on the surface, a payment on one of their myriad of credit cards had been posted one day past due. It was a card he was responsible for. A 38 dollar service fee had been applied to the next month's bill. She provided no other information. No sentiment, no anger. It couldn't even be read as a warning. Just the straight facts. There was something about this text, something encoded deep within its business-like DNA, that made the full weight of his situation hit home. The empire was buckling in upon itself. It had been for a long time, at a glacial pace, but one day soon it would finally cave.

How would he get out from under it?

And did Catharine know too?

Did she understand as she typed out this innocuous text that it really was the end of everything? It impressed him to imagine that perhaps she did know. Perhaps she had crafted this missive with cold, calculated precision, a final slingshot hit that would finally fell the great, wounded beast.

He remained in the stall. He didn't cry. He wasn't angry. His breathing was steady as he leaned against the metal wall, enjoying the stall's close parameters and the strength they seemed to instill in him.

By the time he emerged, nearly an hour had passed.

He hadn't expected to complete the Smart Sani-Saver Montana customer analytics project for another several business days, but the lingering numbness allowed him to lean in and concentrate hard on the numbers and formulas. By four o'clock the sheet was completed. A full week early. It looked fantastic. He dragged it onto the designated folder. It was almost nine o'clock in Amsterdam, but his Dutch boss was in the habit of watching that folder well into the small hours. Was he watching it at that moment? Would he know he had completed the report a whole week early? He turned to Outlook. Sure enough, there was an email from the Dutchman with the subject line, *THANK YOU*. A warm glow hit the base of his stomach, spreading quickly through the rest of his body. He knew he would have to keep things together, professionally speaking, in the coming weeks and months. The empire was beginning to buckle. Stability was needed in order to effectively run the necessary endgame. Compartmentalization. To salvage what was essential and let the rest dissolve into the ether. A captive kingdom in which he could finally truly thrive.

He had forgotten about the cryptic email, but there it was challenging him once again. Now that the report was finished, his courage level had risen. He clicked on it. The only text in the body of the missive was an address in the East Village and a time. 6:00.

He had received his invite.

By 4:30 he was no longer feeling so confident, unanchored and loose since production had wrapped for the day on the rooftop movie set across the street. He felt as if he had come to know many of the crew personally, the guy with the long beard and headset, the girl with the clipboard and plaid shirts, the guy with the pompadour who ran the canteen. In their absence he felt supremely lonely.

General anxiety. It wears down the membranes faster than anything else. The time on the invitation said 6:00. He assumed this meant today. Was he really prepared to deal with this? Perhaps he would be better off returning home to the unmanned gates of the deadening empire, to the spiders in the basement. He thought of the scenery outside the scuffed Metro North windows, a compartmentalized kingdom fading to the chaos and strife of the open lands.

It was now past five. He picked up his phone and keys, dropped them in his pockets, and walked out without turning off his computer.

The subway. What a wonderful thing. He hadn't been on it in years. Rush hour, one commuter standing within inches of the next, everyone in their found spaces, lost inside their own heads, phones out, some with books, staring into space or scanning the ads for plastic surgery and trade schools lining the walls of the train. All of them moving efficiently from their work stations onto public transit and then to their designated, miniscule chambers.

Joy pulsed through him with such intensity his teeth tingled.

Getting off at Astor Place. It was immediately apparent that this neighborhood had morphed in the decade-plus since he had last graced it. St. Marks Place was now lined with high-end Korean eateries. A massive, gleaming gym took up half-a-block on Avenue A. Many of the tenements had been torn down to make way for glass and steel condominiums. He and Catharine had used to come down here and would marvel at the gutter punks in Tompkins Square. There was a foul-smelling dive called Grass Roots where they would have a drink amongst day drunks in wheelchairs. It all seemed so savage and disordered, just a tweak or two away from spilling into chaos.

He preferred this new look.

Coming up on the arranged meeting place, he passed a lanky young man with a flowing beard. The man was dressed in a pirate costume and was holding an acoustic guitar. This individual would not have seemed out of place ten years prior, but now he certainly was, walking with his head down, sheepish amongst the throngs of shiny NYU students and the men in pastel button down shirts returning to their lairs after long days in the Finance District. He felt sorry for the pirate. His freak flag had flown elsewhere.

A red brick walkup between a wiccan store and a neon-lit Korean hot dog eatery. The invite had specified the second floor. The building's front door was open. Inside he found a clean, empty hallway with gleaming hardwood floors. At the end he could see a large room, also empty, that looked like a deserted yoga studio. He wondered if he was in the right place. Then he heard a voice that sounded familiar.

"We're in here."

A small office at the other end of the hall. There were no books upon the wall-mounted shelves, nothing hanging on the walls, just a metal school desk in the middle of the room behind which sat his two new friends. They sat with naturally perfect postures, not the forced kind you often see in people attempting to avoid chronic back pain. Their complexions shone with great health and calm even in the gloomy early afternoon light. They appeared surprised and thrilled that he had shown up.

"Where is everyone?"

The girl laughed. "Who were you expecting?"

"I don't know," he said. "Isn't this some sort of cult or something?"

Now it was the boy's turn to chuckle.

"You won't be meeting any Deserters. You have yet to reach your precipice point. Please have a seat, but only if you wish."

"Is that a good or bad thing," he asked them.

He remained standing. There weren't even any propaganda pamphlets or literature laying around like you would expect with this type of group.

"We don't write anything down," the girl chirped, guessing correctly why he was looking around with what must have been a perplexed look.

"You don't need slogans or guides when you've deserted," the boy added patiently. "You don't need anything specific. You just ARE."

He finally sat, digging his right hand into his pocket. Confession time was at hand.

"This pin came from my daughter's jeans. One of many. I thought it was a jam band or something. I have no idea what I'm doing here. I'm sorry. I'm having some problems."

They both nodded, enthusiastic, as if he had just said something revelatory or profound.

"Please don't look at having problems as a dark thing," the girl explained to him like an expectant mother. "Your daughter must really love you to help you out in this way."

The boy's mop of gold had spilled over his eyes. He brushed it back into place with a quick sweep with his pointer finger.

"Sometimes I wonder if that's true," he told him.

The boy shook his head vigorously and waved his hand.

"She planted a *clue*."

"I wish she would have planted a *joint*."

His hosts didn't laugh, just sat regarding him with a their uniquely blank form of acceptance.

"Ok, yes, perhaps it was a clue of some kind."

They both grinned.

"How would she even know about all these precipice points and Deserters? Is Jennifer one of you?"

"We're a pretty well-known entity," the boy said without a hint of ego or pride, just stating a simple fact. "How old is your daughter and what does she do?"

"Nineteen. Freshman up at New Paltz."

"That explains it," the girl nodded. "Upstate New York is full of Deserters."

He had questions, but a wave of realization knocked them away. It was the combination of his host's glowing complexions, the wide open pours on their faces, and their clear, searching eyes that made difficult confessions bubble up to the surface.

"I don't want to go home."

"Why don't you want to go home, friend," the girl asked only a split second after he said it. Had she known what he was going to say?

"It's a dead language that's spoken there."

They both nodded as if this was a perfectly reasonable statement that they had heard a thousand times before.

"An ancient empire long crushed under its own weight but still struggling to function, going through the motions."

Again with the nodding

"What we teach here is that there is no shame in deserting."

Desertion? He reflected on this for a moment, thinking of deserted families and deadbeat fathers, of men who roll out for a pack of Newports and never return. These types of individuals are reduced to the fringes these days. Shadows are increasingly tough to leave behind. You just can't stamp them down like you probably could in the '50s.

His hosts could sense his distaste at their proposition.

"Deserting circumstances that are killing you is a *natural choice*," the girl explained. "There should be zero shame in it."

This whole Deserter thing wasn't resonating. Is this half-ass message what he had come all the way downtown for?

"You mean like army deserters? I believe they are generally chased down and shot, my friends."

The boy giggled in the manner of someone who had heard something hundreds of times but still wasn't annoyed by it. "Desertion is natural in all wars. It's the only path. What do you do when a situation is quite literally going to kill you?"

"Kill me? War? Look, I know I'm having some problems but..."

"Imagine going on as you are now," the girl interrupted him, insistent but still calm. "Forevermore. Until your death. How does that make you feel?"

He felt himself sinking into the chair. Quicksand. Suddenly hot, he put a hand to his forehead, his fingers singing the taut skin.

Their benevolent eyes, so full of concern. He was sure the girl was tearing up a little. "You can think about it for as long as you need to," the boy told him. "It works best to verbalize it."

The top of his mouth was so dry. He gasped silently for air. His chest cavity felt wrenched, crooked somehow. He wondered if his hosts could tell the full extent of his struggle. Gripping the side of his chair, he concentrated on the tension in his hands, allowing the unease to escape through his palms like two conduits. After perhaps two minutes he finally felt prepared to speak.

"It feels like there's just too much space, too many inches and yards and miles of unincorporated territory...the peripheries have become too broad to manage....overgrowth and savages have taken over...misery....wastelands and gnashing of teeth...oh god..."

He felt strapped in as if to an electric chair, his feet planted firmly on the floor in preparation for the volts.

"And you feel that deserting all of that space is somehow shameful," the boy asked in a soothing voice.

"If you were being poisoned, would it not make sense to stop ingesting the poison if you had the chance to," the girl added.

"Take steps to free yourself from the thing that is killing you," the boy said with increasing conviction.

"Yes, killing you," his partner confirmed.

He finally looked up at them. Could the solution really be that simple? They seemed to inherently understand what he was feeling, his need for compartmentalization, articulating it better than he could. Had others passed through here with the same issue?

"How would it feel to walk away right now? To throw a dying empire of vast space off your shoulders?"

"To *desert*." the boy stabbed the air with his pointer finger, the first sign of aggression either of them had displayed in the short time he had known them.

"I've never even thought about how it would feel. I've been too wrapped up in the dark matters of the present...the realization that it's all gotten so out of control..."

The boy smiled and nodded. His partner let out a short exhale. They appeared relieved at his rambling. He was saying the right things, thinking within the correct patterns. He wondered for the first time if they were lovers.

"Why are you not going home right now," the boy asked.

"Imagine that. Imagine leaving here right now and setting off toward wherever it is that you call home," the girl said, looking him full-on. "Envision it. What does going home look like to you?"

"Death." His voice broke a tiny bit. "It looks like absolute death."

The girl clapped her hands enthusiastically, a move that seemed highly inappropriate to him considering the solemnity of the meeting.

"Then you have reached your *precipice point.*"

She whispered the final two words, savoring the syllables.

"But what about…"

"You. Are. A. Dying. Individual." The boy rose to his feet, aggressively pointing at him with each word. "You articulated this yourself. And a dying individual is no good use to anyone. They flail about, causing confusion, doing their best to take everyone down right along with them."

He looked to the girl. But for what? Her guidance? Her approval? He had no idea.

"Deserting is not about leaving a family."

She remained seated, speaking calmly while the boy remained standing.

"It's about helping them. If you desert, you end up saving everybody."

He felt weighted to his seat, with great pressure on his shoulders, neck, and head. Trying to keep up eye contact with his hosts, he found his vision blurred.

"I've been on the precipice for a long time," he said.

He could vaguely make out that they were both nodding. "You have indeed."

With this, the boy sank back into his seat. His partner leaned forward.

"To make the step is up to you."

The three of them were standing on the sidewalk just outside the building's door. "How can I reach you," he asked them.

"You won't need to reach us," the boy said, reassuring but firm, his eyes glinting in the glare from a streetlight.

A shirtless and surprisingly buff homeless man wielding a rusted-out saxophone let off a shrill burst from the instrument as he passed by. The unexpected noise made his teeth crush together and his shoulders tense up. The boy and girl didn't even flinch. With a panic, he realized he hadn't checked his texts or emails in hours. He had never taken Metro North past the 7:02 train.

"But where do I go?"

At this they both laughed softly, as if he had just hit upon a particularly leftfield punchline. The boy shook his blond mane and turned to walk east toward Tompkins Square. The girl lingered for a moment before following him, beaming benevolently.

"You know *exactly* where you need to go."

Williamsburg. Emerging from the L Train. For ten minutes he walked in the wrong direction, realizing this only when he hit the waters of the East River. Momentarily stunned by the skyline, an angle he had never witnesed from this unfamiliar waterfront in this unfamiliar neighborhood. He stood by a ferry pier between two massive condo high rises, gazing for a full ten minutes at the section of the island around the East Village where the buildings run long and low for miles. Remembering his mission, he doubled back. At the next intersection two bike messengers were swinging their shoulder bags at one another in the middle of the street, screeching, their bikes entangled in the gutter behind a taco truck. Horns blared. Smirking pedestrians filmed with their phones. Two beat cops rushed past him in the direction of the fight. He strode forward without looking back, whistling, his core humming with an energy he had never previously experienced.

And there it was. It was even more magnificent than it had appeared the dozens of times he had viewed it online, a boxy space-aged monolith gleaming under the final traces of sunset. The newest and most massive of all the city's pod hotels, the Williamsburg location currently had nine pods available, the cheapest for $74. There was some sort of medical facility across the street, multiple ambulance lights blazing. A converted warehouse loomed dark and tall to the east. A crowd of extremely loud individuals smoked outside a cluster of restaurants and bars. He passed them silently, wringing his hands as he approached his box of lights. The lobby, its lighting perfectly dimmed under high glass panel ceilings, cocooned him instantly. Two front desk attendants looked up expectantly from their phones. He paused for a moment under the orange pod hotel logo, christened at last.

His check-in time was 11:45 on Friday night.

The next six days were the happiest of his life. Sleep was an art form within the capsule with its blackout curtains, sepia-toned dreams devoid of the hissing sounds and shadow people that had once staked out his subconscious realms, subtle epiphanies revealed to him from a past that never was. They would stay with him upon his waking, never washing instantly away like dreams often do, guiding him through his conscious hours like flocks of soft angels.

A monk on the frontier. Never had he felt so safe and compartmentalized, so free of the dangerous liberties that come with excessive living. He had a comfortable, stylish bed no larger than a prison cot. He had a thick, noise-blocking window that froze Metropolitan Street in its tracks, pedestrians pantomiming conversations and cars accelerating in the sentient silence. Each night at 8:30 a woman in one of the apartments in the warehouse building would stand with her arms folded in front of her lighted window, looking out over the expanse for ten-or-so minutes before turning away. He liked to think that this was a peaceful moment for her, one that she looked forward to throughout her days.

There was a massive flatscreen mounted high on the capsule wall that he never turned on, choosing instead to read the slim volumes of early '60s French noir novels he found himself purchasing, on the merit of their covers alone, from a used bookstore on North 3rd Street. This was the type of store he never would have entered just a week previous. He would have wanted to, but something would prevent him, an invisible but definitive border. He came across it on his first afternoon of pod life and entered without hesitation.

He hadn't read anything that wasn't on an iPhone screen in years. Books from authors with names like Modiano and Manchette that he would never even attempt to pronounce, ravenously devoured back at his pod in the evenings. It got to the point where he would purchase two volumes after work just to make it through the night. There was one that really stood out, so much so that he read it three times right in a row. Titled *In The Café Of Lost Youth*, the novella's actual plot, something to do with an aging Frenchman's longing for a woman he had only briefly and superficially known for a month-or-so, washed over him with little effect. It was the narrator's obsession with quadrants and shifting spaces and neutral zones that mesmerized him. Worlds within worlds within worlds. There were two specific sections, one a paragraph about a vanishing street and the other a long stretch about neutral zones in Paris that were stuck between well-known neighborhoods, that he read back over so many times he could recite them from memory. He couldn't determine if he had entered a neutral zone or was living on a street that would one day vanish. Perhaps both.

There was a glass-door micro-closet which perfectly fit the five dress shirts he had purchased on sale at Men's Warehouse the day after he had dropped out, one for each work day, plus the two black t shirts and two pairs of jeans and slacks he had bought from Banana Republic that same day. There was also a sub-zero mini fridge where he stored the low fat cottage cheese he enjoyed having for his breakfasts. Other meals he would eat out alone, either at a forlorn Chipotle on North 4th Street or the Kellogg's Diner just a short stroll east on Metropolitan. He would read while eating or look out a window. Not for a moment did he miss staring at a television during dinner. His pod also had a cool little frosted glass bathroom that provided everything he needed in order to stay clean and well-groomed. The microspace had grey tiles and space-age shower fixtures and sink. Most mornings he felt as if he was showering in the guest bedroom of a space shuttle.

His pod managed to pack ample amounts of comfort and style into its incredibly small space. Each angle had been meticulously designed, with invisible vents providing the perfect room temperature at all times. No matter where he stood he could reach out his arms and touch both walls, and yet it had the feel of a much larger world. A great expansiveness was alive and slowly unfolding within those 200 square feet.

There was a massive, lush courtyard in the middle of the complex where he sat in the shade of potted trees that weekend. It felt good to relax within this specifically designed recreational space, clearly defined as such, far from the overgrown chaos of all those public parks or backyard ecosystems that needed keeping after. He carefully observed his fellow pod tribe as they did their own lounging around him, tourists just happy to be swallowed for a moment into the confusing maw of the city, business trippers saving money for their companies, backpacker types from the fringes attracted by the cheap room price and most likely cramming four or five fellow travelers into their pod. But the residents that interested him the most were the ones like himself, the solitary ones with the fading features, the ghosts on the faded outskirts. There were a surprising amount of them, easily identified by their shell shocked smiles. They had been through the wars, beaten down by horrific clutter and unorganized lives, only to suddenly emerge into a clinical pureness so precise it nearly hurt. These were fellow new converts to the capsule life. His people. Pod people.

That first week was perfection. Transitioning from his pod in the mornings to the satisfyingly packed subway to his organized office space with its high-walled cubicles, then back to the subway to the bookstore with its alphabetized shelves and on to his pod which had been cleaned and disinfected in his absence plus provisioned with new towels. Then it was a neat, predictable dinner at Chipotle or The Diner and on to reading in his perfectly-lit and temperature-controlled capsule and into another round of ultraviolet dreams.

The pods were not conceived with long-term residence in mind. For this reason the pod life necessitates switching locations each week. After that magical first week at the Williamsburg pod hotel he switched to the 39th Street location, the site where he had initially reached his precipice point just over a week prior. His pod had the exact same space and amenities as the previous one, only everything was reversed from left to right. This small change was nonetheless monumental and seemed to morph his new space into an even more vivid dimension. It was a five minute stroll to his office, but he did miss the subway. The customers at the 39th Street pod hotel were quite different. There were no backpackers and no touring indie musicians. There were still lots of Euro travelers, but these were older and obviously untroubled by the burdens of maintaining cutting edge fashion sensibilities.

On the margins, lingering like a familiar dream, there were still his fellow pod people, just like he would see at his next pod location and each one after that. At the 39th Street location there was a 30-something professional-looking woman he would pass in the lobby or outside on the street as they came and went. He recognized it in her face immediately, the stunned sense of freedom at having cast off domestic weights, uncontrolled realms, an entire dying empire. On the Saturday after he moved to the 39th Street pod hotel he saw her in Bryant Park, sticking to the shade and sipping a vivid green smoothie with a contented smile. Then there was the man with the NYCHD bag he noticed in the continental breakfast lounge on two consecutive mornings. An NYC resident and city employee on the run within his own zip code, only blocks but many worlds removed from daily clutter or domestic strife or more esoteric tortures. These early pod pioneers never outwardly communicated, passing like spirits in the halls of an abandoned mansion, but were so easily identifiable they could sense one another's presence. He felt it every time he passed one in a courtyard or in the hallway or on the street outside, the psychic antennae of a growing pod legion.

It took only a couple of days to come to an unfortunate realization. The stinging disorder of the outside world did bleed into the pod life. But there were easy fixes for many of these wayward splatters. For example, after several vicious texts from Catharine regarding his mail piling up, complete with photos of mail stacks on the table in the hallway, he made the point to switch all of his monthly bills to electronic only. The stacks in the hallway would no longer haunt him. Then there was the stable address issue. What would he list as his main address on work forms, applications, 401Ks, etc? The pods could not be listed as permanent residences, but this was solved by acquiring a PO Box at the Varick Street post office.

A quick glance online revealed a number of pod people support groups popping up in major coastal metropolises across the US, and even more across the rest of the world, especially throughout Asia. There were three groups in New York City alone. Two of them, "Pod Life NYC" and "Pod People Unite" took place once per week, and the other, "Pod Movement", fell on Saturday afternoons and regularly drew dozens. A number of message boards were popping up as well. The first and most popular was TribesOfThePods.com which boasted hundreds of members and thousands of individual posts per day divided between topics both practical ("Space Utilization Thread") and esoteric ("Possessions Cause Psychic Damage?"). Other boards were more specialized, some focusing on specific locations (Berlin Metro Region had two) and others dedicated to the various factions and sub-factions of pod people that were beginning to form. There were smaller, situation-based boards for recent divorcees and domestic breakup victims and a board for until-recently broke individuals who had just landed jobs in the city. Then there were two boards for the type of pod person he was, both of them quickly filling up with existential musings about decaying household empires and the psychic trauma instilled through their chaos of excess space. He never posted on these boards or attended any of the meetings, but he found the numbers comforting. The pod tribes were rising.

One of the main concepts preached on the existential boards was that a pod convert's abandoned family would certainly never understand. He found this to be only half true. It took roughly 24 hours after his conversion for Catharine to reach him by text. Her missive was both impersonal and vaguely scolding, like a boss checking in on an employee who was more than 15 minutes late. He hit CALL instead of TEXT. Amazingly, she picked up. She sounded highly distracted, a mere apparition on the far radar of his orbit. One heavy breath and she would be lost to space.

She didn't sound surprised at all. Her breaths on the other end of the line didn't fluctuate. In many ways she sounded bored, as if he was reading off a grocery list. He told her *exactly* what he was doing. The pods. The compartmentalization. The dead empires. The chaos and the clutter and the long, binding shadows sprung forth from their fixed postal address. None of these aspects seemed to interest or mystify her in the least. He didn't blame her. When spoken aloud into open air they were blunted in their impact, the restrictions of language dulling the vibrancy and swagger they carried in his head. She was more interested in the specifics of their relationship. The straight facts. Had he left her? Should lawyers be involved? Was there another woman? And if so, then who was it? It seemed of utmost importance to her to know if it was someone from work. Her rapid-fire line of questioning caught him off guard. He hadn't conjured pre-planned answers for any of them. He'd been so hung up on the existential elements of modern freedom that these small details hadn't even occurred to him. He knew from the forums that a pod person must distance themselves from the petty concerns of outsiders, but hearing them ringing from Catharine's mouth he had a sickening feeling that it wouldn't be that easy. His silence, his abject lack of answers, didn't seem to infuriate her. Slight annoyance, yes, but no discernible fury. He realized then that this is how you know when your marriage is over. When the fury is gone.

"I need you to sign Jennifer's tuition form for next semester. I'll DocuSign it," she said, matter-of-fact, as if this was the lone reason for their phone call and they had just managed to get to it after some inconsequential formalities.

"Don't worry." She sounded on the verge of laughter. "You can sign it digitally. Right from the comfort of your own pod."

He imagined her stalking the halls of that massive house, looking around in appreciation. Although his hand had begun to shake, still he felt safe in the knowledge that he was no longer in the violent winds of that polar vortex.

True to her nature, his daughter was more accepting.

Catharine must have let her know the situation. She called on a random Wednesday night from New Paltz while he was attempting to organize his clothes in the space-efficient manner a long thread on one of the pod message boards had recommended. In contrast to the lacerating cynicism wielded by his wife, Jennifer seemed genuinely curious about his new pod existence, tossing out a series of well-placed questions about everything from a pod's basic layout to philosophical and ideological queries about the concepts behind them. She seemed cold to their imminent empirical collapse. Jennifer most likely already knew it was a lost cause and that it always had been.

"This thing with Wheel is really making life here uncomfortable," she whispered as if she were afraid the hippie wannabe drug lord would emerge from a utility closet in the dorm hallway.

"Why do they call him 'Wheel'?"

"You know, after the Grateful Dead song?"

"Oh. New Paltz. Of course. Was never much into them. Too many notes."

Silence on the other end.

"Or, well, maybe that one track about some sort of wolf…"

"Dad, snap back into focus here. I think Mr. Wheel might actually *do something* about this debt."

He said the following before thinking:

"Well then I'll do something about it first."

A surprised exhale on Jennifer's end.

"It's like I'm speaking to a real human being all of a sudden."

The setting sun through the pod's window had caused a long orange cylinder to streak across the floor and wall, temporarily distracting him.

"You have to compartmentalize your troubles," he told her before she clicked off.

His performance and time management at Smart Sani-Savers was more efficient than it had ever been. There was a marked increase in production, with customer data deep dive reports being completed several business days before they were due. His Outlook inbox was empty by the close of each day. Although his boss, that distant Dutch enigma, hadn't outwardly said anything, he could tell that the man was impressed just from the tone of his emails. In several of these missives he had been asked what he was up to over the weekend or that evening instead of simply being ordered to "have a good weekend/evening". Good vibes radiated from the very Calibre

11 font the man utilized. He could feel that a promotion was now closer than ever. Executive Analytics Associate. He whispered these three words to himself while walking the streets or staring into space on the subway. Executive Analytics Associate, over-and-over like an incantation.

He kept his eye out for his two angelic saviors, often lingering in the break room for longer than he had to in hopes they would float in. He microwaved his lunches an extra minute, until they were bone dry. He filled cups of coffee, dumped them out, then poured more. He splashed around in the sink. Still they did not appear. Which was just as well. He came to the slow realization that he was looking for them simply because it seemed like he should be, not because he actually wanted to. He didn't need them anymore. He didn't even know what he would say to them if they crossed paths.

Often he doubted that they ever even existed.

As the days of his new life accumulated into what felt like a solid foundation, text contact between him and his daughter picked up drastically. Jennifer kept him abreast of some of the more pressing matters of the empire, such as the fact that Catharine was worried he would stop paying his half of the mortgage. That month he made sure to wire the required funds to her account as he had always done before crossing over the precipice.

Finally, on the 19th day after his retreat into the pod space, he received a formal-sounding Gmail from Catharine requesting that they meet up for lunch. She would be in the city for a meeting the next Tuesday. He knew that Mary Ann Liebert often sent her to editorial board meetings in depressing hotel conference rooms in Manhattan. She had complained about this many times when he was still living within the empire.

He felt surprisingly little trepidation entering Faux Taco on 33rd Street. His breathing was steady, his steps in line, no trembling in his hands. It felt no different than meeting up with a colleague for a brisk lunch to talk business. Which is essentially what this was.

"There are 97 more payments left."

This was the first thing she said to him after a brief, eye-contact-free" hello". She was speaking of the mortgage. He didn't think it was that many, really, more like 56, but either way what did it matter? It would never be paid off. He had accepted that years ago. She never had and never would. But she looked great, more relaxed than she had in a long time, possibly ever. The scowl creases that had crept in around her mouth had smoothed out considerably. The pods could most likely take full credit for this. With him gone she had less to scowl at.

"We'll make them. Until we die, that is. Either way it doesn't matter."

She winced as if in pain, shaking her head lightly while laying a napkin across her lap.

"It does matter," she hissed under her breath. "It matters *very much*, as a matter of fact."

They had once conceived a human. Now their eyes couldn't meet. They had once tried acid and spent the night clinging to one another in a shed, both of them convinced that the trees outside housed evil spirits. Now her distress didn't faze him in the least. The crushing weight of their unruly empire had snuffed out all feeling. He had fallen beyond it somehow. She was still in it. This was just her way now, while his was the way of the pod. In the days since he had left he never once doubted that he made the right decision.

In that moment he was sure of it.

"So you're really doing this? This is your thing now? This is what I have to tell people?"

She bit off the tip of a piece of bread with vicious chomp. He shrugged.

"Nobody can be this insane. You *must* be up to something."

The accusation would have affected him had there been even a hint of emotion behind it. But there was nothing. A stage actor in a bad regional theatre production running through her lines. She was glad to have him gone. Her only concerns were peripheral.

"Has Jennifer been around the house?"

And there it was. A fury bubbling up from behind her eyes that made the skin on her cheeks tremble. Real emotion. It had always been that way with her about Jennifer. She had been furious with her daughter since the very first minutes of her birth.

"She's been back twice. Just for a night each time. I don't know what's going on with her. If she fails out of that school I swear..."

He waited for her to finish. She swears what? She'll kill her? She won't stock the bathroom with her fave conditioner? She'll rename her after her worst fear?

She didn't finish her thought.

"Has she told you anything," she sighed, clamping her eyes closed for a moment.

"No," he said too soon, nearly cutting her off. Her eyes flashed suspicious. "She doesn't say shit to me. Ever."

"Join the support group," she sneered as a waitress with insanely white, bleached teeth approached.

Later, after their food had been ordered and eventually delivered, her eyes suddenly flashed clear fury again in the midst of his story about the movie shoot on the roof across from his office. She hadn't said anything in some time. He had been rambling on about inane matters, just to fill in the edges, before she cut him off.

"You can walk right on out of my life," she seethed in a possessed, low hiss. "I don't care. But you should never, ever, abandon your daughter."

She had slashed out with a hidden razor the moment he thought all was calm. He knew she had gotten him. He wasn't sure where or how badly, but soon the blood would reveal both. And he knew it would be a long recovery. Still he was glad that she had done it, soothed by the pain's sudden rush. It was the only hint of true feeling she displayed during their business meeting, which lasted just 45 minutes. This is all the time it took to discuss the practical matters which needed tending to. They had run out of things to say to one another by 12:40 and were just waiting out the check. Their plates had already been cleared, hers half-full and his scraped clean. His appetite had been massive over the past several days as he acclimated to his new surroundings. By 12:45 he had paid the bill. They parted on the street with light waves but no physical contact.

"I won't abandon her," he had told her as she walked away.

She didn't turn around.

Perhaps she hadn't heard him over the din of the traffic.

For the third week he switched to Pod 51 off 3rd Avenue, where his pod happened to have a partial view of the East River. The pods in the 51st street location were 15 dollars more expensive than the first two pod hotels he had inhabited, but this was paid back to him in the form of the space age entrance that made him feel as if he were entering the bowls of a seedy spaceship, the roof deck with the sweeping cityscape view, and the pool tables in the lounge where he would play by himself some nights. He also spent a lot of time on the roof deck in the suffocating late summer heat, gazing out from a designated recreational area over geometrically gridded streets. Compartmentalized bliss. Everything in its right place.

By his third day in this new pod complex he had begun to notice a fellow pod dweller who was often lounging in the searing heat of the roof deck at the same time. On two occasions they were the only guests taking advantage of the massive deck. The tall, handsome African American man, somewhere in his 50s, seemed relaxed and serene, lacing his fingers behind his head as he stared off at the point on the horizon where the cityscape touched the clouds. The two of them nodded to one another the next morning as they passed under the lunar lights of the lobby. It was a knowing, instinctive gesture executed without eye contact, one that would become very familiar to him over time as he ran across other pod people in other lobbies and designated recreation areas in other pod hotels. He wondered what the man's handle was on the pod forums. Is he "PodGuy777" who always complains about "tourists" who book one night in the pods just to check them out and then vanish from the scene? Or is he "BrotherRay" who has been banned several times from a couple of the forums for ranting about government surveillance of the pod culture? ("They want to keep us weighted down in debts and every-day maintenance worries. Don't you see? By dropping out we are THREATS!") But no, this guy was far too centered to be BrotherRay. He saw him again that night out on the deck where it was cooler than it had been and suddenly crowded. The sunset cast orange light shards off his shaved head. The man finished his quite good gin and tonic from the downstairs bar (they took orders on the roof), folded up his MacBook and slipped it into a case, and walked away without seeming to notice him.

Setting up a FaceTime meeting, not just two word texts with multiple emojis, with his daughter proved to be as difficult as gaining an audience with a highly-protected and hyper-paranoid tribal warlord. It took them over a week to lock in on a particular night, and even then the time was changed at least three times last minute.

He had only used FaceTime once previously, and it took him several minutes to figure out how to make the thing switch on. When it did, he was stunned to suddenly be confronted with the smirking, shockingly adult face of his daughter. Her face and head had evolved over time, taking on finer hair and losing the greasy imperfections of the early teen years. She wore light makeup and her lips were fuller. Already there were some grin lines along the side of her mouth. Echoes of her mother. Layers and layers of ghosts. A cinderblock dorm wall behind her made him think of the goth posters that hung on the similar wall of one of the two girls he had dated in college. Siouxsie & The Banshees and Christian Death. The wall behind his daughter appeared to be blank. Was she not planting roots in the outer world? Would no one recall the walls of her dorm in a melancholic rush 20 years from this point?

"So, let's see you new world," she demanded.

She made him sweep the laptop around the pod so that she could take a look. It touched him that she was as curious about his realm as he was about hers.

"It's like that scene in *Spaceballs* where they escape the exploding ship in little rocket compartments," she exclaimed.

Then she wanted to see the roof. In the elevator up to the deck an ancient Chinese couple regarded him strangely as he held the laptop aloft, speaking to the screen. On the roof he moved the device around so she could take in the expanse of skyline.

"You're like a kid," she said to him when he finally sat down in a quiet corner away from a group of tourists smoking a foul smelling joint under one of the massive potted trees.

"I'm not mad at you for saying that."

He was worried others on the deck could hear him, but spoke up anyway so she could make out his words over the reverse vacuum of the city din.

"But please know this isn't some whim. This is a perfectly orchestrated move. This is the compartmentalization of a life."

Her face in the screen had the look of concentration she used to use when attempting to read the older children's books in the store when she was still a toddler.

"I get it, Dad. You don't have to explain it to me. I support you. I really do."

There was a sincere edge to her voice that killed the need to explain further. He was relieved for this since he had been having trouble articulating it fully in his mind.

"And you understand about me and your Mom and I take it…"

She let out a giggle.

"Um, yea Dad. Of course I do."

There was a sense of jadedness in her voice that made him sad. How long had she sensed it? Had it ever bothered her?

"You guys are like hostile business partners. Time to liquidate that shit and branch off. I am taking Intro To Biz, you know."

He had seen countless movies and television shows where daughters and sons would freak out upon the Big

Announcement, screwing their faces, smashing things, spouting the most vicious of names. He wondered when she had become so icy and understanding. So French. It really was a thrilling development.

She jumped at a sound in her background, lurching forward as if she were about to be hit with something. He jumped as well, but she immediately smiled and smoothed out her hair. "Just a shroom freakout in the hallway. Happens all the time," she shrugged.

He coughed and nodded.

"This situation with Wheel has reached a whole new level," she said, suddenly deflated. "Now he has his townie drug squad on the case. This guy Spence. Some bitch Fawn. What type of person is actually named Fawn? They've been asking around town about us. They have people working within the University. Townies toiling as groundskeepers and on the kitchen line. They can get to us. They really can."

"All this over what? A few hundred dollars?"

"More like a thousand. These people are from Kingston, Dad. A grand is like a year's rent there."

He was momentarily distracted by sharp pangs of laughter ringing from the Eurotrash tourists with the joint.

"Just because you think you have it all architected, just because you're in the midst of some grand transition," she said, seething now. "Doesn't mean the rest of us do."

"Who is the rest of us? You and Catharine?"

"Please, Mom's fine. Too fine, really. That woman was born beneath a shark star."

Some small remaining pangs of fatherly instinct told him to scold her for referring to her mother as "that woman", but the concept of a "shark star" had him too thoroughly dazzled to say anything.

"She can survive the waters. I can't. Not *these* waters anyway. And if you can't help me, then what good does all that compartmentalization really do?"

He noticed a shadow move on the far left corner of the deck, the less popular corner devoid of the river view. It was the man he had been noticing, his fellow pod pioneer, who had been sitting quietly on a post-modern deck chair but had risen to stretch. He kept his back to the people on the deck, looking out over the confusing tangle of city quadrants.

"I'm going to help you," he told her, surprised at the conviction ringing through in his voice.

The guy checked his phone, his face momentarily aglow in the digital light, then headed for the elevator vestibule which was all lit up like an alien greenhouse in the center of the deck. He gave a single nod as he passed.

"Sorry to end this thing on such a grim note," his daughter said. "But I really hope you can."

Leaving the pod early for work the following morning. He wasn't feeling the usual rush of optimism that went hand-in-hand with exiting the climate-controlled pod on the way to a subway compartment that would transport him to his designated workspace. He was properly rested. There were no outward threats antagonizing him. But something was off. He couldn't fall peacefully in line with the commuter rhythm, remaining mysteriously and profoundly troubled all the way to his stop. While purchasing a six dollar iced coffee from a place called Caffeinated Moon, a woman in her 30s waiting for her drink, cute and clad in casual office wear, gave him a quick look and a smile.

Dear god.

He hadn't even been thinking about that sort of thing. How would an individual like that fit into the world of the pods? He walked out of the shop without acknowledging her presence. Commuters walked close together on the street. Something was still off. He felt their pain and neuroticism clinging to him more than usual, intruding on his personal headspace like wasps buzzing close past his ears.

The swarms receded once he was safely enmeshed within the structured confines of his office building. Super Sani-Saver, the saviors of all saviors. He typed away happily on the spreadsheet, South Dakota customer data steadily filling up the columns. At one point, while heading for the bathrooms he thought he saw the Precipice Point Girl standing in the break room with her back to the door, but when he entered all he found was a gaggle of temps with angular hairdos and purposefully wrinkled dress shirts sitting at one of the tables watching a video of a rapper with multi-colored dreads toting an AK 47 while standing through the sunroof of a moving Suburban.

"Can we help you," a girl with Buddy Holly glasses asked with a slashing, acidic tone to her voice.

"I don't think you can."

As the late morning inched along the spreadsheet began bothering his eyes. He spent an hour watching the action on the movie set across the street. A chase scene was being shot. A muscular man with a shiny, shaved head and tight-fitting white v neck t-shirt was made to run the same ten steps over and over again, at least 15 times, as a camera on tracks swept along next to him.

The swarms eventually made their way back.

The bi-weekly-paycheck tension of the office, the panic of monotony, seeping through the white office walls as he ate his lunch alone at his desk with the door closed, humming into the long, dragging hours of the afternoon. The swarms followed him down the subway stairs, staying with him as the train creaked to a halt between stations and stayed there for 20 minutes without an announcement. Fellow pedestrians on the streets. He sensed their decaying frames, too much caffeine and screen time and too little sleep, gliding past him, vessels of disillusionment.

He browsed the French fiction section at McNally Jackson even though he had three novels back at the pod that hadn't yet been cracked. Out of the corner of his eye he thought he saw his fellow pod pioneer from the rooftop and lobby, wearing a massive fedora, in the Nordic Literature section. He ended up purchasing a book solely for its cover, a cartoon cat with devilish eyes and a serpent's tongue. He hit the street feeling better, the temporary rush a purchase brings, the swarms fading.

Opening the book on the train, the first line caused all the blood in his body to rush to the head.

"There are certain streets that attract so many ghosts that they become spirit entities."

Walking up 51st, a spirit street if there ever was one, nearing the pod hotel. Some raw instinct from deep within his psyche told to make a sharp left into a high end watch store. He stopped dead just within the entrance, long enough to light up the faces of two eager sales team members prowling the floor, then quickly turned back towards the door. A man in a fedora nearly collided with him, rushing into the store like a mother frantically searching for her wayward child.

It took him a moment to fully realize that he was the wandering child in this case. And the worried mother? It was his fellow pod dweller.

"May I ask why you've been following me all day?"

It was strange to see the man's face outside the glow of an iPad on the darkened pod hotel rooftop or under the rows of space age fluorescents in the lobby. The harsh light of the outside world rendered him far less handsome. Grimacing defiantly, it appeared as if he wanted to say something but no words came forth. A tinge of fear. What were this guy's intentions? Was he about to be cut or shot down in the entranceway to a hip watch store? The guy nodded out the door in the direction of the pod hotel across the street, its lobby compartment looking uncharacteristically dull in the relentless late summer afternoon shimmer.

"Let's get a drink," he said, turning for the street.

He didn't even need to ask where these drinks would be poured, following his new friend in the direction of the pods.

It was close to 100 degrees on the pod's designated rooftop recreation area. They sipped the tall, glistening gin & tonics that had been served to them by a surly tender with the Yankees logo tatted on the side of his neck.

"I can tell that you're a very practical dude, so I'm assuming I can just be straight with you."

His pursuer sipped his drink, loose and casual, as if hanging with a friend he saw once-per-week.

"What makes you think I'm practical," he asked the man in a slightly offended tone.

The man took off his fedora and adjusted his sunglasses. His bald head glistened in the sun.

"Because I've been watching you. I can see what you're up to with…" He swept his hand over the length of the pod hotel. "…all of *this*."

He was starting to get the feeling that this guy wasn't a fellow pod dweller as he had assumed. He wasn't on the run from any empires. It was an interesting feeling that hit him sideways, made the tips of his ears burn, a feeling it was a struggle to immediately identify: betrayal.

"You're simplifying your life right down to the bare essentials. Kind of like a luxurious monk. Limiting your options to just one semi-plush cell."

The man raised his eyebrows, welcoming an interjection that never came.

"I can dig it," he nodded in respect.

"It's called compartmentalization. This kind of thing is big in Japan and…"

"I was impressed with that move you pulled back there," the guy cut him off wearily, his forearm muscle rippling as he clutched his drink. "The fake-out at the watch store? I wasn't expecting that at all. I can't even tell you the last time a mark caught me."

Now the man was glaring at him with a begrudged respect. It struck him for the first time that his pursuer could actually be quite dangerous.

"I surprised myself too. I'm telling you, this pod life has opened up whole new chasms for me. Wait…I'm a mark?"

"Indeed you are, chasm boy. I was hired by your wife."

He nodded. This should have been a revelation but it landed with the dullest of thuds. Oh, Catharine, had it really come to this?

"She gave me the whole story, bruh. I know many things about your marriage. But don't fret. It isn't anywhere near as strange and disappointing and…well…*disturbing* as 96% of what I see. And by that I mean I won't be talking about your marriage with my fellow PIs over beers nine years from now.

No, not your marriage. But we will definitely be discussion YOU, however."

"Where do PIs hang out," he wondered out loud, picturing a dark dive with some sort of high stakes card game going on in the corner and hockey on the TV screens.

"We drink amongst you." He raised his glass. "You'd never even know it was us."

"But I knew you were following me this afternoon. You aren't that slick."

He waved his hand dismissively. "We'll see about that, motherfucker."

They sat in silence for a moment.

"Anyway, you're soon-to-be-ex-woman gave a whole dossier-style tip sheet on you. Your whole weirdness with this pod shit…and believe me this is some weird-ass shit right here and I can't wait to get up out this bitch…and of course she isn't buying it completely. Cath thinks it's all a front. A smokescreen. A lie. The first instinct is always adultery, of course."

He thought of the woman in the coffee shop.

"I'm not even thinking about women right now. It's never been about that. I…"

"Ummmm…" He cut him off. "She actually assumed you'd be with a man. You haven't touched her for years, my friend."

He considered this.

"It'll take me at least five years of weekly therapy to come to terms with that assumption. How late do therapists see patients? It has to be after five…maybe Tuesdays…but it's actually pretty touching that she would be so concerned about there being someone else…"

The man finished his drink with a harsh sip, grimacing.

"It's far from jealousy, my man. What, are you dense or something? She wants to *divorce you*, friend. If you were gay or cheating that would be easy. But no, instead you had to go the hard way. The crazy way. A quest. A revelation. That's tougher right there. That makes it complicated with the courts. With her friends circle. It makes it look like she's abandoning a partner with mental issues."

He flinched when the words "mental issues" were spoken.

"So I'm considered crazy now by the greater society just because I wanted to scale things back a little? Downgrade a bit?"

"Scale things back? That shit's crazy right there. Downgrade? *Downgrade?* This is America, motherfucker. 'Downgrade'. That's the only word the court would need to hear. 'Oh yea, he's deranged, the poor man.' They'd rule against her in a heartbeat. She's a monster for leaving you during this time of obvious mental illness."

This was a lot to take in. He realized his drink had been finished but he didn't recall drinking it.

"So she hired a private investigator to prove I'd left her for…a man…just so she could have a sympathetic sob story to post on Facebook?"

The guy shrugged, obviously bored.

"I knew within minutes that you were clean. Or, well, there *was* that moment with that honey at the coffee shop…"

"Wait, just how closely have you been…"

"…but you're quite possibly the most upstanding tail I've ever had the supremely boring misfortune of being assigned to."

Was this a compliment or an insult? He wasn't sure, but it hit him like the latter.

"Is this some sort of trap within a trap within a trap? Are you even supposed to be telling me all this shit? Isn't this conversation a violation of some long upheld PI/Client confidentially code? Perhaps Catharine should have done some better research in choosing who to hire to follow my every boring move."

The guy let out a startling cackle, his eyes flashing with mischief.

"The case is over, my dude. As of now, today. It's closed."

A grave sense of professional pride bled through in his voice. He paused, thinking out the right words to paint the confession he was about to reveal.

"No offense, but I don't like your wife all that much."

Despite the odds that had multiplied between them over the years, he still grew instantly defensive of Catharine. His shoulders tensed. The man sensed this.

"I know, I know. People grow apart and these things turn into business partnerships more than anything. I've seen it thousands of times. Literally. But I gotta' tell ya' I've *never* seen an individual as fully *checked out* as her."

He nodded at this. Checked out. This was indeed the correct descriptor, but it applied to both parties in this case. Somehow this professional observer had missed his complicity.

"Don't get me wrong, you're no lotto hit or anything," he conceded, seeming to sense what he was thinking. "But think about it. Her dude just left her ass to live in some chintzy 200-square-foot closet and her main concern is a checking account that's never had more than five grand in it."

He waved his hand dismissively at his new PI friend.

"She can have it."

He nodded and smiled, holding up a tiny iPad.

"Of course she can. But she won't be getting any help from this report."

He pointed at the device.

"I'll be telling her you're as sexless as a eunuch at sea."

He thought about this.

"Eunuchs go to sea?"

"You *really have* run off to the pod circus," he said in an amused manner tinged on the edges with wonder. "The story holds."

They were looking at one another. The man obviously expected him to say something, to defend himself or launch the first volley of a philosophical debate. But he said nothing and the PI just shook his head, whistling lightly through his teeth.

"Unbelievable, my man. Unbelievable."

It was sweltering on the rooftop. Beads of healthy-looking sweat had broken out on his stalker's head. Shards of sunlight glinted off the windows of the surrounding buildings. The city expanse beyond the rooftop was still and shimmering, stunned, for once, into silence.

"And you want me to what? Thank you? For reporting… the truth?"

The man shook his head. He wasn't understanding something.

"It doesn't always go down like that. Sometimes I gotta' tell these clients what they *want to hear*."

"Well that's unethical…"

"But you? I like you."

The guy reached across the table and gave him a stinging slap on the shoulder.

"You're the best kind of mark. Not just another dude in love with a singer/stripper. You aren't even *rare*. You're an *original*. I'll be talking bout you at PI happy hours til the day my liver takes its last breath."

He held out his arms, framing the scene, his eyes clamped shut with great relish.

"The man who fled the nice house in Westchester and the fairly hot wife to live in a fuckin' transient pod."

He opened his eyes, beaming.

"Hey, you're making it sound more insane that it really is. It's not a crazy concept at all. It's actually pretty logical…"

"Oh, it is, man. It is," The PI conceded, scowling in thought.

He wondered how he managed to sit confident and upright in the direct blast of sunlight like that. He himself felt like a wilted vegetable.

"I suspect this'll be a growing fringe, to be honest. I'll probably start seeing more of these cases. It's just that you're the first one. And the first one is always very special."

He placed his hand on his shoulder in mock affection.

"I did my research, man. I'm not some hack. I know how they roll in Tokyo and places like that. Hell, man, in Hong Kong and shit people disappear into the pods all the time. It's impossible for their families to trace them. Those things are just built up to the sky in that motherfucker. Obliterating space, maximizing square feet. You're on to something early, my man. Micro-efficiency will one day be king. People will move like refugees, with very few possessions, sleeping in space age tombs."

He regarded him, his eyes wide with new vision, like a curios exhibit in a pop art gallery.

"They'll be free," he whispered to the PI, who kept looking at him with the same bewildered expression.

"Look, man, can we move to the shade or inside? I'm dying here."

His stalker ignored this.

"I'm really not sure about all that, fella."

The PI was lost in thought, not moving to wipe the sweat beads from his forehead even though they were threatening his eyes.

"People have opposing definitions of freedom. Some would say that freedom is a thousand square foot yard. Maintaining that yard is just an aspect of maintaining freedom. It isn't a shackle."

Fury. A charred scent around the synapses, sparking to the surface as it only does for a true believer.

"How large is *your* yard, man? I bet you don't have one. I bet you don't know what it's like to be shackled to…"

"But I'd say that you pod people are definite pioneers." He continued his one man conversation. "Pioneers of what, exactly? No idea. But this shit will catch on for sure. There'll be women jumping on board soon, looking to get away from basic-ass husbands and wiping kiddie snot off the drywall."

An enormous smile now spread across his face.

"This'll be a major windfall for me. I'll be tracking you pod motherfuckers all the time in ten years. You just gotta' look to Asia. All this shit starts there. The 'anti-marriage/romance/procreation' trend over there had me worried for a second. All that cuddle café shit. That would kill my whole job right there. But no…I'll get my check off all the suckers already locked in."

His eyes grew wide with the revelation. He leaned forward.

"When they flee to the pods, baby."

He backed away from his overly shrewd new friend. Business instinct. It always turned him off.

"I'm glad people like me will be making you a living," he said sarcastically, although it had no effect on his stalker. The PI sat in triumph in the direct sunlight, no doubt thinking of all the cases that would be flowing his way due to the oncoming exodus of pod freaks.

"All are welcome in the pod kingdom, my friend. Even private investigators…"

This got his attention.

"Hey I get it, my man. I really do," he said, looking him straight on for the first time. His eyes appeared to be bloodshot.

Had he been nipping booze all day? Pills? It must be boring to have his job, trying to grasp a bunch of thin souls afloat in the wind day after day.

"I've been staying in these pods the past...four? Five?... nights while tracking you."

He didn't take his eyes off him, hammering the table on the words "past", "five", and "nights".

"I could get into this. Them rooms is small but comfy. I've been sleeping better. The fitness center isn't bad. All for ninety a night. That's less than fuckin' rent if you play it right. This is where I'd probably be if the wife finally booted me. Clear my head. Get my shit *compartmentalized*."

Three pigeons strutted past them, two scrawny ones flanking a massive bird with a blue head and blank eyes.

"The service could be better, though."

He shook his empty glass. The PI nodded.

"I could use another drink myself. On me?"

"It better be. You just made, what? 5 grand off this case?"

His new friend grinned mischievously.

"And all I had to do was mirror your boring-ass routine for a few days."

He slapped him playfully on the shoulder with a cupped hand, adding, "you're not that bad dude..."

"Aw shucks. Hope I ain't blushin'."

"....for a mark."

"I'll take that."

The man was gone for what seemed like a long time. He sat in silence for all those minutes, pinned by the sun, the heat, the skyline that looked like an oasis in the haze. It startled him when the PI sat back down, the clink of the glass as it was placed before him on the table.

"Now that you're assignment here is a wrap," he said to him. "Perhaps you can help ME compartmentalize the one last thing that I need put in order."

The next week he was right back where he started in the Williamsburg pod hotel, solidifying an undefined circuit, like closing out a circle drawn on water.

Still the ventilation systems hummed efficiently, whispering of contentment and gilded engineering deep within the systems, right down to the guts. The floors remained solid under the step, betraying no hint of give or collapse, not a creak or groan. The room was similarly spotless, so modern it could have been a capsule within a pioneering space colony, a lush and all-enveloping exile.

He couldn't help but look for signs of decay, any developing chinks in the infrastructure, evidence of intrusion from the chaotic and unrestrained realms just beyond the thick glass windows and the intimately-lit front desk reception area. Running his fingers across the surfaces within his new pod, they never came back caked in dust. When checking in, he glanced behind the desk to check for misarranged files, paper sediments, trash and soft drink cans left strewn about by the workers, but there was nothing that concerned him, just spotless postmodern surfaces Windexed clean, mounted iPads with the "pod" logo emitting their warm glows, a lone functional table with nothing on its surface.

But why was he searching for flaws?

Up until that week when he returned to his original pod precipice point, there hadn't been a single taint of doubt. Not once since crossing over did he question the basic structural elements of the pod existence or theorize about potential safety breaches. It was the steady, forward strides of the true believer that carried him through his days. There was no need to question a concept that had already proven itself to him through easily felt waves of security and comfort, with tangible results such as a regular sleeping schedule and a clarity of mind so alien it was tough to get used to.

Still there were no doubts in the concept of the pods, just a black streak of suspicion that the cluttered outside terror scape, in all its empirical invasiveness, would easily locate it on their insect-like sensors and move in to crush it. The pods went against everything they stood for; Spartan strength, minimalist thought, freedom of movement, non-consumptive mind-frame. They would want it dead, desecrated, reduced to ash and bone. They would plant thorn bushes amongst the rubble so nothing could ever grow there again.

A major attack would always be preceded by subtle infiltrations, passive provocations, and was these that he found himself on the lookout for during that week when he returned to the Williamsburg pod hotel.

Although he saw no outward signs, still he couldn't shake the thought. Somehow the chaotic outside regions would have to co-opt this space. Nothing was beyond their reach. A last vestige of order within an enveloping vortex. It just had to be doomed. But where was there to run after the pods? In dreams he had seen sleeping bodies being slid into single file rows like in a morgue, and the vision comforted him greatly. A flash from a distant but perfect future.

In the nighttime hours he would look through the postmodern slats that lined the pod's windows, and in place of the north Brooklyn cityscape he saw mortuary style residence buildings stacked to the sky, just beneath flight path level, with rows upon rows of sleeping slats lining each wall. As the minutes passed this ultra-convenient and space-saving skyline would fade back to the same dull urban hum, the same jumble of mismatched buildings beyond the touch of zoning regulations. The transformation would creep in slowly but with a finality that was beyond concrete, and all he could do was take it and try to breathe.

And each night there was the woman.

He had gotten to know her presence during his first stay at the Williamsburg pod hotel, when he had just crossed over from the embers of his dying empire. She lived in the factory building on the corner that had been converted, like many of the industrial buildings in the immediate vicinity, into condominiums. Her hair was either brown or black, it was hard to tell through the humid, mid-September haze that lined the tops of the buildings in the nighttime hours that week, and was sometimes worn loose and flowing to her shoulders and other times tied back. It was also tough to make out her facial features, let alone her specific expressions. All he knew about her was that she would appear in her lighted condominium window each night at 8:30 and would stand with her arms folded for around ten minutes, a stern centaur looking out over a land she clearly resented but nonetheless must protect. Then she would would abruptly turn her back on the expanse, her shadow moving out of the window's frame. The light would turn off seconds later.

On some days the woman in the window was his only solid reference point to the world beyond his pod, his subway car, his office. Her image would linger with him throughout the days. He never guessed at her life or her name. He didn't care if anyone else was living in that condominium. All that mattered to him was that she took those ten minutes each evening to look out upon the expanse outside her window.

It would have been hopeless to guess what she was thinking about in those moments, demeaning, like fastening a shackle to a dream. He often thought of her in the minutes before he fell asleep, an angelic outrider on the edges of his thoughts, helping guide him toward six or seven hours of delicious sleep within his blacked-out pod. Perhaps her ten minutes of gazing out upon the cityscape each night was what held the whole thing in place, kept it all from sliding into the same vortex that had swallowed all else. If nobody else was grateful, then he certainly was. He hoped that she could sense this somehow.

The serene watcher of the slipstream.

On Thursday of that week, for the first time, he was beginning to doubt the pods. It wasn't his decision to flee his dead empire that he doubted, nor was it the pod aesthetic he had been enchanted with from the start. It was simply the small but consistently nagging feeling that his preferred new territory wouldn't be sustainable in the long run. There were whisperings on the message boards, entire threads stretching on for many pages, with various pod people chiming in with their interpretations of impending doom. Some said the governments of the major world powers, fearful of the growing mass movement away from home ownership and what it would mean for the markets/consumerism/capitalism, would eventually move in to shut down the pod hotels. Others claimed that shadowy surveillance agencies would become wary of these new tribes of rootless citizens, nomads by choice whose fluid living patterns would throw up hardships for those who wished to keep daily track on each citizen, and new laws and regulations would be introduced that would severely cripple the movement.

Other threads speculated that the pod life would become a hip new trend amongst 20-somethings, meaning the pods would be booked solid for months on end and consistently rising in price. Out of all the threads he obsessively clicked through, this was the one that seemed the most plausible. Everything good eventually gets co-opted. Already he was seeing pod tourists, usually in groups, who had stumbled upon this niche world on the deepest dregs of the internet (usually on 4Chan, where the obscure trend was looked upon with equal parts fascination and ridicule), and were passing through to check out the scene. He would see them standing outside the lobby with their luggage, waiting for their Ubers or Lyfts, talking to one another out the sides of their mouths as if they didn't wish to be overheard by the pod natives. No doubt they were discussing the fastidious strangeness of the scene, the cultural implications, with the same curious smirk he would witness cross their faces as they wandered the halls or the lobbies or the roof decks or posing for selfies in the hip eatery that had sprung up on the first floor of the Williamsburg pod hotel at some point during the three weeks he had last graced it. Already the rates were beginning to rise on weekends, and the forums were alight with various strategies for circumventing the bad net results of a growing popularity and a fair amount of doomed talk that outright depressed him. Often he would click his laptop shut whenever he read a post about how the pod life as their small tribe knew it would soon be coming to an end.

But what would he do if the pod network failed? There was no returning to the dead empire, that was for sure. There were many new possibilities and theories espoused on the message boards. Some spoke of building their own pods on owned property outside the cities where the pod hotels existed. Others talked of entering monkhood or suicide. Flush in the still new glow of his defection, he ignored it all the best he could.

Ignorance. Wasn't this what had originally gotten him deep within the empire trap? Blind allegiance and docile passivity? Would it once again lead to his doom? He thought of this on Friday as he looked out the office window, scanning the rooftop where the action movie had long-since wrapped up production and moved on, leaving behind large mounds of the trash they had been using as props. Fake trash transitioned to real trash. Janize was in the office for a change and had been ignoring him the best she could at her desk by the window. He didn't hear her the first time, so she practically shouted to get his attention.

"Are? You? Ok?"

He didn't answer, but he knew he wasn't ok. There was something loose in the foundations of his new world. The whole thing was just too good to be true. There was no getting around it. You can switch living quarters, but the devils are still going to come around for the rent.

That night he waited for her.

It was the first time he had done it. It would also be the last.

By 8:00 he was watching her darkened window, waiting for that light to come on. The minutes passed so slowly that when the light finally did spill over the frame, when the woman took her cross-armed stance to survey the panorama outside her condo, it was an anticlimax. Just the same scene he witnessed every other night. He tried to make out her face but the distance was too great and the lighting too poor. A shadow figure, slender and vague, riding out the wavelengths of some other realm.

Was she smoking?

He thought he saw her bring something to her lips, but she could have just been yawning. Either way he wanted an answer. He sensed that this being understood somehow. She was trapped within her own empire, gazing upon those who had been exiled. Was it better where she was? Or should the exiles ride it out even in the face of diminishing returns and constant inconveniences, forever paranoid but hugging a basic principle?

He waited. He watched. The woman stood as still as ever. The only thing he could make out was that her hair was down. Finally, as always, she turned sideways in preparation to kill the light, to return to her anonymity. Just as he would be returning to his. He waited, nearly hyperventilating, for her light to go out.

But tonight was different. Already she had lingered in the window longer than usual. Instead of immediately flicking off the light, she turned back to face the window. She seemed to be leaning forward. The blood was pounding hard in his head and chest. His earlobes grew hot and his back ached. He placed his forehead against the thick glass of the pod window, surprised by how cold it was. He didn't take his eyes off her. Did she see him? Had he been outed? A lone voyeur in a sea of lighted windows? The woman straightened up. She held out her hand. The gesture was deliberate, staged, and she held it for a full minute. Even in the grainy distance he could recognize the signal, hand-up, palm forward. The universal sign for "halt" or "don't move forward". Then the light switched off.

She was telling him to stay.

It was the first time he had been outside the comfort of the pod/subway/office pipeline in quite some time. That instantly familiar, cold hand of death felt its way up his spine as the houses and lawns and trees and chaotic parks and shopping strips took over the scenery north of the city, gaggles of teens skateboarding in empty parking lots, witnessed through the passenger side window of a black Suburban. His former stalker hunched steady and emotionless at the wheel. He wasn't the one being stalked anymore. The PI was now *his*.

He knew he had to get himself together, to stamp down the oncoming nausea. He'd been in the pods for too long. The scenery, familiar but vividly ugly, hit him like a splash of cold water to the face in the midst of a deep sleep. It was like coming out of a Fentanyl fog when the pain of your injury, dulled for some time, comes roaring back into focus.

The PI, whose name was Corey, was listening to Vanessa Williams at a soft volume. He didn't have the heart to ask him to please turn it off. They were making their way Upstate.

"Headed for the hinterlands," the driver said, acknowledging his passenger's discomfort with a knowing smirk.

At one point, within the first 30 minutes of the journey, they passed the two exits that would have taken them to the gates of his former empire. There was a brief flash to the day he and Catharine had passed the same exit in a rented car, following close behind a moving truck. He remembered how uncomfortable he had felt on that day. But it was already in motion. He had stamped it down, but you can never bury something deep enough. Like a shard of glass lodged in the skin that eventually makes its way to the surface. The body rejects it.

The vegetarian eatery on the main strip of New Paltz was done up to look like a diner but served no regular coffee and the plates were more expensive than Manhattan or even

Williamsburg. In the booth behind Corey, two dudes in thrift store plaid and beanie caps were having a heated conversation. "Trey's been dead for over three years," one of them was saying, his eyes burning with a true believer's conviction as he chewed on a green burrito. "We're not sure if it's a sophisticated hologram or an imposter clone, but we'll get to the bottom of it one day." Outside on the street two girls were unsuccessfully attempting to hula hoop. A large jar at their feet was labeled, "We need a miracle." It was nearly full of change and bills.

"Their fathers alone probably clear half a mil per year each. Stepdads? Even more." Corey the PI had several printouts spread on the table. He hadn't touched his tofu meatloaf sandwich. From these papers a slight but impactful cache of information was gleaned. Wheel's real name was Micah Reichel. Micah Reichel's residence was at 11 Clinton Avenue in Kingston. When stating this address, Corey the PI had shaken his head and muttered, "Dear God, man." Micah Reichel was at one point, several years prior, a full-time student at SUNY New Paltz and had grown up in Glen Ridge, New Jersey. There were two arrests on his record; a simple assault and underage drinking four years prior and a possession with intent to distribute one year later. The latter charges had made the local papers. *Paltz Dorm Drug Ring Busted.* Corey had several printouts from social media pages as well. A Facebook account that had been dormant since the narcotics distribution arrest and his eventual expulsion. A beaming, broad face. Expressive eyes. Fine blond hair slowly transitioning into a classic hippie shag, high school jock muscles transitioning into flab. Lots of party pics. Lots of photos with arms around various friends. Lots of String Cheese Incident T-shirts. All flowing and free.

Once the printouts were pushed aside, Corey the PI, who had been narrating them in a robotic, bored tone, said, "Now we get to the real shit, partner," with some relish. "This Wheel dickbag started out just purchasing for personal use. Molly. Blow. Eighths of kind. There's a white trash townie drug crew, here in New Paltz and this Kingston mostly, that supplies the school. Has for 30 years. Harmless, really. Lots of the kids get to know them, apparently. But this Wheel kid? He *really* got to know them. He got in with them quick. They recognized something in him. Some little prick from the Jersey burbs, just passing through for four or five years like the rest of them, but he was just born with an instinct, you know? Like I was born with an instinct for this shit." He swept his hand over the stack of printouts. "And you were born with an instinct to live like a space monk. This kid was born with the DNA of a small market drug dealer. The second he met them, it was just *on*. Lil' guy slid into the classic 'middle man' slot. A plug. The guy the Paltz kids knew to go to. He took their cash. Dealt with the townies. Got them their shit. Because who wants to deal with townies, really?"

As if on cue, a two-tone Accord with rusted out wheel bases rattled past on the strip with a shirtless, generously tattooed man with gray pigtails hanging half out the passenger side window attempting to keep a shakily fastened ragged couch from falling off the roof.

"Before long our homeboy Mr. Wheel had quite the booming little business going. This explains all the thrilled "friends" in those old soc med snaps. But he was taking a bit off the top, naturally."

One of the hula hoop girls was now speaking with a kid wearing overalls with no shirt and a long, greasy ponytail. The other hula hooper continued gyrating, waving "hello" to passing cars. He wondered how Jennifer managed to fit into this unique ecosystem.

"And where's the printouts on all of this?"

A wide grin from Corey the PI.

"This the type of info right here you don't get from any printout. This is reading between thin lines. This is intuition."

He took a bite of a bitter-tasting kale salad, nodding as if he understood all this PI jive.

"Think about it. That bit of intuitive story building leads us right to the next solid fact we have, my friend. The infamous dormitory raid. It's right there in the paper More than 20 kids snatched up. All Mr. Wheel's fault, of course. They do this all the time, the cops. Since Wheel lived in just one of thousands of dorm rooms in the building, they went and classified it as a building sweep. Tore up every room. What the media classified as a "SUNY Drug Ring" was nothing more than 19 kids with bongs in their closets and one guy who knew a bunch of townies."

"Knowing townies *is* pretty messed up…"

"*You're* pretty messed up, Pod Man. Anyway, after his inevitable expulsion, it would appear that instead of running back to the Jersey burbs to live off Mommy and Stepdaddy, Mr. Wheel instead did something unprecedented. And this makes me have some respect for the guy. At least he's keeping it interesting."

"He went into academic publishing?"

"Even worse," Corey the PI took a dramatic sip of his unsweetened iced tea. "He went full-on townie."

"Oh shit."

"Within months lil' man was moving weight right along with the guys he was buying from all those semesters. Maneuvering through the ranks. Finessing contacts. Three years on and he's one of the top seven dealers in Ulster County, which is really saying something out here in these hippie woods.

College kids with disposable income. Hopelessly unemployed locals. Ancient hippies who never lost their tastes for the underground. It's the perfect mix for a healthy drug trade, my friend."

"They never mentioned this during parent/student orientation day."

"Our boy has kept himself pretty admirably out of the police clutches during his little run. We've got that possession with intent. Weed and some Hydrocodone pills. Reduced to misdemeanors. Pled out. There's that drunk in public/fighting thing back when he was still a student. We've also got a dropped charge on a domestic violence issue..."

At this he gave him a glance.

"There's two warrants out. Nothing they're gonna' kick his door down for. Wheel never coughed up the fine on that intoxication charge. Our boy also has to take care of all those parking tickets. 2002 Red Honda Civic, by the way. Oh, and it looks like he was under investigation for a statch charge last year but nothing came of it."

"Wait, does statch stand for..."

"Don't get all vigilante dad about this."

"But..."

"Outrage doesn't suit you."

"So being worried about my own daughter doesn't suit me?"

"You can be worried." He shuffled the papers, refusing to look at him. "But the whole *father on a vengeance quest thing* doesn't ring true with you, man."

He was studying him closely.

"You're more...cerebral."

He nodded at this, convinced at his own insights.

"The type who would move into a pod hotel for aesthetic purposes."

"You can stop the analyzing any time."

Corey the PI laughed at this, thumping the table twice, loudly. Several heads in the vegetarian diner turned.

"Oh, I'm done. Believe me, you're not that interesting. Anyway, he's definitely on the radar of the local po-lice. But not under surveillance or anything. Not that they even have the resources to put anyone under surveillance..."

It was the first time he had thought about the pods since they had sat down for lunch. He felt safe in the relatively cramped diner-tube layout of the restaurant. For the entire ride north he had fretted at the sight of all that anarchic open space bleeding out past the Suburban's windows. The town had struck him as disordered as well. There was too much leeway, too much space between the houses, too many yards. The side streets appeared deserted even on a sunny Saturday. Unoccupied space, the untamable wastelands, the devil's stomping grounds.

"Mistah' Wheel's social media has gone dark since he crossed over. This is normal for movers and shakers shaking their way up the chain. It's a smart move, really. The opps watch social media closely."

"Must suck to have *that* assignment. Lots of pictures of food to sift through."

"Must suck indeed, my friend. I've managed to trace a couple of recent-ish shots of our boy, though..."

He extended his phone. On the screen was their Wheel, still handsome and sporting the same barrel jock build, only now exhibiting definite townie drug dealer traits; a smudged-looking tattoo creeping up the side of his neck and a sparkly, platinum grill that made him look like a grinning robot. In the pic he was standing in front of a large bay window half-covered by a bed sheet, beyond which a grey strip of sky and snow-covered yard could be seen.

"Our boy seems to have cut himself off from his family within the past couple years."

At this he gave him a quick glance.

"Why'd you look at me like that? I'm not cutting myself off from *my* family, just from their...entanglements."

He held up his hand to stop the onslaught of words.

"You're on an existential trip," he said. "It's a different dimension entirely. Our man Wheel has done gone and volunteered for a dour, desperate existence."

"He's gone full townie."

Corey the PI nodded solemnly.

"Never go full townie," he said.

Standing outside the diner in the sunshine. They ignored the hula hoop girls begging them for change. Corey the PI was glancing nervously up and down the strip. Many a ratty vehicle rattled past, small rusty trucks and old Saabs. Inspections must be lax upstate. He wondered if Wheel himself occupied any of the vehicles going past; Making a delivery. picking up some cash, on his way to intimidate an associate with an aluminum bat, perhaps just picking up some almond milk.

"I'll be needing to draft in some help today. We'll be dealing with Midtown Kingston characters, after all. So it'll be 500 for the day."

"You said this was free, Corey..."

"Oh, *I'm* working for free, but Brig certainly isn't."

"Who in god's name is Brig? You're drafting in some sort of muscle?"

"This is lower Clinton Avenue, G. Special circumstances."

"Jesus Christ." He surveyed the strip they were standing on. "Aren't all these Upstate hamlets the same? Quant little hippie woods enclaves? Headshops with tie dye peace signs and Hendrix posters in the windows? Organic brunch spots? Outdoor antiques markets? Glass blowing classes?"

Corey the PI smiled while hitting a button on his keychain to unlock the Suburban.

"Midtown Kingston ain't no Woodstock, my friend."

A three story Victorian house set back from the roadway in the woods, a little worse for wear but impressive against the trees and sky, elegance ingrained in its many-decades-old structure. A large trampoline with a safety net sat in the too-tall grass that covered the front yard. This is the problem with houses, he thought. The wilds are constantly striving to reclaim them. All was still and quiet until Corey the PI let off two short, sharp blasts of the horn. A tall man emerged from a screen door on the side of the house less than a minute later. He approached the Suburban with business-like strides, his glasses glinting in the sun. He looked very much like a guy headed off to work.

"Corey," Brig nodded upon seating himself in the backseat of the Suburban. He grinned respectfully when introduced to his boss's passenger. In the rearview mirror he could see that his new conspirator had the appearance of a college professor, glasses with clear frames and a neat grey goatee, his hair swept to the side in that aged Rimbaud look often adopted by academic types. The man eased back into his seat. His face betrayed no hint of interest at what the mission ahead would hold.

"This is your muscle," he whispered to Corey the PI as he backed out down the gravel driveway.

He grinned widely at this."

"Are you my muscle, Brigsey," he called to the man in the back, who chuckled to himself while staring out the window.

"Mr. Brigs here is more source than brawn. A spiritual navigator, if you will."

Brig nodded at this but said nothing.

"A spiritual navigator of what, exactly?"

"Of the Upstate underground."

At this, Brig tipped an imaginary hat, grinning proudly.

"This the Pod Man," he asked Corey the PI, cocking his thumb toward the passenger seat.

"In all his glory."

The Suburban was moving at a high rate of speed on the empty road shrouded by trees. Glints of sun through the branches gave the world a jagged, abstract edge.

"Brig and I met on a case. Or should I say, Brig was the *target* of this particular assignment. The first one I ever had up here. Some local involved in a criminal enterprise we won't be getting into…"

"No we won't," Brig muttered.

"Brigsy here was in some serious debt, wasn't you? And in hiding too, weren't you?"

Brig shook his head in sorrow at the memory.

"Until this asshole tracked me down." He nodded to Corey the PI. He still hadn't made eye contact with the passenger.

"I ended up liking him so much, I never turned him in," Corey the PI laughed.

Brig let out an incredulous breath through his nostrils.

"You saw a guy who could help you with cases up here. That's all you saw," Brigs said with some venom detectable under his laidback drawl.

"You've never turned down the cash, have you Brigsy? You need it too, don't you, Brigsy? After being disbarred and all…"

"Disbarred? This guy's a lawyer?"

"*Was* a lawyer. The 19th best defense attorney in Ulster County. And you could pay him in blow!" He grinned affectionately at their passenger in the rearview. "Remember those days, Brigsy?"

The man waved all this away as if it were nothing more than a bad suggestion.

"Four years sober as of last month, bitch," he stated triumphantly. "How bout we just go ahead and get this over with, shall we gentlemen?"

Corey the PI laughed.

"Where do you think we're going right now? A jaunt to get Frozen yogurt? I liked you better when you were on the shit, man. You're all jumpy these days, Brigsy," he said, still grinning at his employee in the rearview with much affection. "Looking great, though. I could just kiss you."

He made a smooching noise. Brig flipped him off.

"I knew this dude would be an asset in breaking the market up here," he nodded toward the backseat. "Probably defended every bit of pond scum at the bottom of this here lake."

He swept his arm across the road ahead. This was an opposite world to that of the pods. They were passing through a small village made up of three or four crumbling houses and, for some reason, about nine laundromats. It wasn't fear that crested within him. It was sadness. All this chaos and waste. All these individuals lost.

"I paid off this local wannabe Scarface myself. Now Brigs works for me," Corey the PI was explaining, pointing to their passenger as if he were a piece of furniture or some other household possession, a centerpiece of sorts. "He said he was just in til he worked off what he owed me, but now the guy's on the payroll. He just can't get enough of Uncle Corey, can he?"

In that moment it appeared that Brig had indeed had enough of Uncle Corey, and had so for many a moon.

"About that," Brig said. "I'm gonna' need more than 500 for today. There's an added Kingston fee…"

"Talk to the Pod Man here. He's payin' your way today."

"That's a factor we still need to work out," he reminded his new PI friend.

"Oh, Brigsy here is worth every thin dime. Believe me. As a matter of fact, if it wasn't for Mr. Brigs there's no way we'd be able to track down your transient-by-choice mark today."

Something about the word "today" stirred him. There was action happening. And it was all going down in the coming hours. Situations in life. You never recall exactly how you fell into them, and you never have a clue about how to get out.

"We're on our way to find Mr. Golden Grills…now?"

His heart began acting up something major. Just that morning he had awakened in a perfectly controlled cave where nothing could possibly touch him. Now he was at the mercy of the wilds.

"This is maybe the last time I'm doing this, Cor," Brigs was whining behind him. "Rita and the kids think it's pretty sus that I'm 'having brunch' all these days. They know nobody wants to have brunch with me anymore."

"That's for sure," Corey the PI nodded. "I certainly don't."

They had passed a sign several miles back that read: *Kingston 5 Miles*

"So this is what you do," he spoke out the side of his mouth to their ever-nonchalant navigator. "You get assigned to cases and then take in the people you're investigating? People like Brigs back there. And now me. And how many others?"

"What can I say," Corey the PI shrugged while stretching out his neck. "I collect lost souls."

Corey the PI looked him dead on, serious for once. The urge to demand that he please keep his eyes on the road was eradicated by the sincere light clouding his eyes in that moment.

"This is *your* trip. We're doing this for *you*. It's a *quest*. We're compartmentalizing the loose ends of your life."

He found himself nodding involuntarily.

"Don't you see?" He veered onto the exit for Kingston without even looking. "All this can be tamed. This whole anarchic expanse. Don't ever fear it. It's all just an extension from the core. You can pare it down, man. Organize it. The whole thing ain't nothing but one big pod."

Kingston. On the outskirts it could have been any town; two-pump gas stations, combination Taco Bell/Kentucky Fried Chickens, abandoned-mini-strip malls, Asian massage parlors with "24 Hours" stamped on their windows. In just minutes they were on a strip not dissimilar to the one they had visited in New Paltz, only this one was post-apocalyptic. There was a long-dead theatre with its once-ornate exterior in shambles. A small colony of sidewalk dwellers, some in tents and boxes, others camped out on blankets, had set up a permanent-looking civilization underneath the marquee overhang. Any business that wasn't a convenience store or liquor outlet was shuttered. They passed several well-designed parks that were overgrown with weeds, darkened in mid-day under a canopy of free-willed trees. Lone figures sat upon benches, staring into the haze. Corey the PI swerved to avoid a woman in a red sweat suit who had walked out into the street and fallen on her knees at the center strip, her arms outstretched to the sky.

"See? This is what happens," he whispered to Corey the PI. "This empire has fallen."

"The Uptown section is very nice," he countered, a demented real estate agent, as he passed a folder back to Brig. "Coffee shops and fusion restaurants for miles, baby. Somethin' tells me we won't be seeing it today. That's not Mr. Wheel's kind of hood."

"You said he was from North Jersey…"

"He rejected it. He chose this. This is the world he thrives in."

There was a well attended domino game happening on the lawn outside an old folk's home. Someone had wheeled out a tray of food which was being ravenously devoured by a large flock of pigeons. Brigs whistled lightly trough his teeth while inspecting the papers.

"Yea, I know him. Wheels, right? Dumb jock student turned Ulster County Golden Triangle member. I don't blame him, really. A more exciting existence, for sure. The chicks have less teeth, though."

"Wheel. Singular. You repped him back in the day?"

"Never stood next to him in the docket. He had too much money to get stuck with me. But he stopped by once when shopping. Bullshit statch charge. Girl had a fake ID. I'd have gotten him off. Ended up with Borrel on that one. Never made it close to trial."

"What's our boy like?

"Funny. Likeable. That two-car-garage upbringing still shines through. But he's got a lot to prove because of that. These sharks around here would want to stand him down. Pull up on him. Test him out. He's not one of them, not really. So he's gotta' be ten times as fucked up as they are just to get by."

"And what would Mr. Wheel's intoxicant of choice be, Brigsy?"

"Tweaked. For sure."

"Oh boy. Makes sense. Helps him adapt. Armed?"

"You know it. And in the worst way, too. He's got the tools but has no idea how to use them."

Corey the PI smirked at this.

"Looks like we're in for a good one today, Pod Man!"

He slapped him on the shoulder.

"We are now officially WAY above my paygrade...."

"But this is your mission, pod boy. This is your daughter. This is how you compartmentalize your existence. This is how you make the WORLD your POD, brother."

A loud sigh from Brig in the back.

"That's what this is all about? Wheel's got this guy's daughter tied up somewhere?"

"Not yet,"

Corey the PI winked, his eyes flashing, clearly relishing his role as ringmaster of this unwieldy circus. He turned back to Brig as they sat at the stop sign of an empty intersection.

"So what type of crew does Mr. Wheel In The Sky Keeps On Turnin' run with? All upstanding young gentlemen, I take it?"

"He's named after a Grateful Dead track. Not Journey," he corrected him.

Brig turned to face him for the first time.

"And just how would *you* know something like *that*?"

He was clearly offended that his monopoly on small town drug dealer trivia was being challenged.

"My daughter told me."

Corey the PI was beaming.

"His daughter told him, Brigsey. Looks like we don't need you on intel for this one. You're out the car at the next light."

Brig waved this off.

"Fine by me. There's a bar two blocks over. If you order a Miller Lite it costs twenty dollars and has a little bag taped to the bottom."

Corey the PI shook his head at this, lowering his sunglasses to regard his back seat passenger in the rearview.

"I thought you were off the white horse, my dude."

Brig shrugged under the withering glare. "When in Rome," he said, before letting out a deep sigh, getting down to business.

"Anyway, let's see, Mr. Wheel Is Turnin' By The Grace Of God is probably gonna' be chilling with my good friend Kale, as in the too-bitter superfood, a young man whom anyone that hangs out around the courthouse or county lockup knows real well. Wait til you get a load of this one, Cor. White rasta, only he goes for the militant Peter Tosh thing over mellow Marley vibes."

Corey the PI scratched contemplatively at his bald head, maneuvering the Suburban onto yet another desolate street full of once grand, now abandoned houses.

"You mean like that dancehall shit? Like Vybz Kartel?"

Brig was shaking his head emphatically.

"Like guns and PCP-laced joints in the name of Jah, my dude," Brig explained. "Our dynamic duo have gone halfsies on some cases. I've repped Kale before. He's a vegan, needs a shower, hits a miracle with the occasional slumming Uni chick."

At this they both shot him a nervous glance.

"He's part of the chain that supplies all those trippy kiddies in the dorms," Brig continued after missing a beat. "Right there with Wheel. Originally comes from some trailer park up in the wilds of Phoenicia."

Corey the PI scoffed at this.

"What's with white people and trailer parks, man? And then they always got a boat sittin' out front. If you can afford a boat, you can afford a motherfucking apartment."

Brig rolled his eyes.

"Thanks for the social commentary as always, Cor. Look, I'm not dead certain those two even roll together anymore. But

I scored off Kale Salad a couple times back in the day and he's a little 'touched by the Gods', if you get me, so tread carefully."

He looked back and forth between the two men in the front seats.

"I don't care about Pod Man here but if you get murked then I'm out a gig."

"I'ma' stop fucking around with this back woods shit real soon, so you'll be out a gig anyway," Corey the PI let him know.

"Oh, and there's a couple other things you should know about Wheel and his bad news bears," Brig cut him off.

'There's more?'

"Oh yea," he confirmed. "Wheel and Kale roll with some Aryan bro types. I don't have any names, but I know they're linked."

"But dude's a white rasta," Corey wondered, screwing up his face.

"Aryans got that meth hookup, Cor," Brig explained as if to a particularly thick student. "Ideals have nothing to do with it."

"Word…," Corey the PI nodded thoughtfully. "Ok so college dropout townies, white rastas, neo-nazis, anything else we should be aware of?"

He had turned off onto a side street lined with colorful hippie-looking houses, a gentrified block with large oak trees that almost completely blocked out the sun. He enjoyed this new block immensely. The feel of the enclosed space helped him breathe a little easier, although he was having a hard time adjusting his vision.

"Oh yea, you better hope Piss isn't around…"

"*Piss?*" Him and Corey the PI asked at the same time.

"Oh yea, Craig Pistman," Brig said as if speaking of a wayward but loveable second cousin. "Basically lives at County.

Can't control himself, really. One of the last cases I handled. Got him off on a battery rap. Down in New Paltz. Punched a college girl right in the face at some bar. She was underage and had nine E pills on her, so her parents made her drop the charges. Piss has a long history of smacking up the SUNY kids, actually."

Again they both gave him a glance.

"Any women or brats in the house, do you think," Corey the PI changed the subject quickly.

"Was just about to get to that," Brig, clearly in his element, continued. "They call her Fawn. You know, like the baby deer? Not sure if her and Wheelie are an item or not...but Fawn's been fawning around for a while. Her parents own the most successful health food emporium in the area, which is really saying a lot considering the area. They live in a beautiful con-verted church out in the sticks..."

"This is the sticks right here," Corey the Pi interjected, pointing out yet another row of crumbling houses.

"Sticksier. Out in the deep woods," Brig said. "Anyway, their Little Fawn flew the coop years ago. Got taken in by the Wheel crew. She doesn't deal or anything. Just chills out and trips and snorts and whatever. She chopped into some guy's ear with a sword last year. An ex-colleague repped her on that. Poor lil' thing got six months. Pretty sure she'd be out by now. So watch your ears today, kiddies."

The Suburban had eased into a neighborhood where the houses were set far back at the end of long, narrow lawns. The structures had obviously once been solid, brightly painted, Craftsman-to-the-core, but had endured at least a decade of mismanagement and neglect, and in some cases willful destruc-tion. The branches of interior trees peaked out from boarded windows, hundreds of empires collapsed into one another, reclaimed by the forests. Soggy brown bags and abandoned strollers lined the strips of lawn. Small groups gathered on various porches, glasses and bottles and chains glinting in the sun, staring the Suburban down. In that moment he longed to hear the two sharp clicks the doors made at the pod hotels when locked.

"Hey man, why do I have to be along for this," he asked Corey the PI. "You're the private investigator, after all. I should be safe in fully-functioning Manhattan while you take care of this shit."

"I already told you twice."

The driver held two long, smooth fingers aloft.

"This here is a favor. I don't roll alone on favors. It's your mission, your pilgrimage. I take people where they need to go to fix what they need to fix. Therefore, you must ROLL."

He caught a deep sigh from Brig in the back. The man had obviously been through this same scene many times previous.

Walking the long lawn of the house Brig had pointed out to them, it occurred to him that these were the perfect dwellings for those who lived outside the law. Any visitors had to walk the gauntlet. You could see them coming for minutes in advance as long as you remained alert. He made sure to walk behind Corey the PI, who didn't seem nervous in the least. Brig had remained behind in the Suburban which was parked around the block. Corey the PI had asked him to be "the eyes" of the operation. Brig had nodded at this while sliding into the driver's seat. The engine remained running. Brig had dialed in to Corey the PI's phone, which would be kept on speaker during the mission so he could listen in. He was impressed with the trust the PI had for this Brig individual. The man could have driven right off at any point.

The house looked like most of the others on the street, only in a bit better shape. This empire had only recently fallen. It needed painting but the structure was sound. Dead grass on the lawn. Six windows on the front exterior, two covered with bed sheets, one with an American flag, one with a Jamaican flag, one with a *"Don't Tread On Me"* flag, and the other with a strip of tie-dyed cloth with *String Cheese Incident: Red Rocks 2001* stamped on it. All was quiet on the block, though there was the sense that people were watching from somewhere. The house was silent. Perhaps no one was home.

He was surprised when Corey the PI rang the outside buzzer, a traditional move which seemed entirely out of place in these circumstances. There was a long minute during which Corey the PI whistled lightly to himself with his hands clasped behind his back like a visiting salesman. His accomplice had no idea what to do with himself, kicking at a clump of weeds next to the low-slung concrete stoop. He half-hoped nobody would answer.

He didn't know what he expected to happen when the door opened. Guns blazing? Explosions? Cannons and bayonets? Instant hand-to-hand combat? Anything but the door just lazily swinging open like that. Corey the PI's expression didn't shift an inch. If anything he was bored. A tame assignment, just a side trip to pass the time, doing a little favor for some freak he had taken a liking to.

The yawning young man at the door was definitely Wheel. Within the past hour he had been shown several photos of that face. And there it was in the dusty dark of the vestibule, still handsome with pronounced cheekbones, but thinner now and with some damage around the eyes. Bad diet. Lack of sleep.

Dehydration. Worry. His daughter's tormenter was buckling under the weight of the empire he had chosen to build.

It took him a moment to notice the weasel perched on Wheel's shoulder. The animal had white fur and untrusting red eyes that darted back and forth in its narrow skull. The creature shifted to the kid's right shoulder to get a better look at the visitors, it's tiny claws gripping and stretching Wheel's white v neck tee which exposed his still in-tact muscles and neck tat, which upon closer inspection turned out to be a crescent moon. He was barefoot and sported baggy button fly jeans. His eyes were sleepy and blue. He yawned, seemingly unsurprised to find two strangers at his door.

"No offense but you boys don't look much like rastas."

He gave them both a quick glance, from their feet to their heads, smirking. "Now do they, Samantha?"

The weasel made a short, sharp screech and curled into a ball on his shoulder.

"Look, we didn't burn up their bales, man. We wouldn't do that. We *respect* the sacrament. It's bad-ass karma to do such a thing."

He opened the door wider, dim light coming from somewhere in the dank interior.

"They sent *you two*? I didn't think them boys dealt with anyone who doesn't walk with the Jah, man. But whatever, do what you gotta' do. Put me out my misery, man. It's been a pretty shitty week.."

"What in God's name are you babbling about there, Wheel," Corey the PI spoke in a calm voice loaded with endearment. "And you mind keeping your hands out of your pockets, friend?"

Wheel withdrew his hand from his pocket as ordered, removing a crushed-looking joint and accompanying lighter.

"You believe this, Sam? They come to *our* property and try to order *us* around," he addressed the weasel out the side of his mouth while lighting the joint. "That's some rude shit right there, fellas. Nobody has any manners anymore. Look, if you aren't some sort of dread head hit men, then you mind telling me who the fuck you are and producing some badges or identification or something?"

For a moment he wondered if Corey the PI was going to say anything. Was he going to have to speak up himself? The thought terrified him. How does one slip comfortably into situations such as this? Fortunately for everyone involved, the PI snapped into focus.

"We've come to pay off a debt," he said matter-of-factly. "A relatively small one that you shouldn't have gotten so hardcore about. Though I'm sure you won't mind having this one off your books. One less thing to harsh your vibe, right Wheelie?"

Exhaling a massive cloud of chemical-smelling smoke that definitely wasn't weed, Wheel looked to the sky and cackled. "So The Dirty Merchant finally pays up, huh? And he couldn't just come settle this shit himself? Two years hiding out up in White Junction for what? Two grand? Tell Merch I don't want his cash. Tell him to come *talk to me*. Tell him I just want him *back in my life*."

Wheel was suddenly emotional. Even the weasel appeared disturbed. Corey the PI extended his palm as if to comfort an emotional child.

"Nobody named Dirty Merchant sent us, Wheel. We don't need to know about your personal life. Look…"

"Waaaiiittt," Wheel said, squinting suspiciously over Corey the PI's shoulder at his other visitor. He put one hand to his head, pointing at him with the other.

"Are you that dude who roadied for Levon?"

He began wiggling back and forth in the doorway as if he had to urinate.

"Look, man, that dude is *dead*, ok? I don't owe anybody shit on that. This business stops at the *grave, man*."

Withering under the fire and brimstone glares of both Wheel and his weasel, he held up his hands in truce.

"I'm not working for anyone named Levon," he explained slowly, enunciating each syllable. He was suddenly suspicious that there was someone else just inside the door in the folds of the house's dark interior fringe. There was music coming from somewhere inside.

"Iron Butterfly? Seriously?" Corey the PI laughed. "Look, brother Wheel, can we just get this thing done? The man here isn't involved in your lumpen hippie dream. He's just tryin' to compartmentalize his whole life is all."

Nodding vigorously, Wheel sucked hard on the synthetic joint which half-vanished with the inhale. His blue eyes, which would have been dreamy had they not appeared so disturbed and vacant, studied him closer but this time with something resembling respect.

"A man on a *quest*, Sam!"

Wheel exhaled an impressive plume of foul-smelling smoke which the weasel, perched on his shoulder, greedily breathed in.

"Well." Wheel lightly kicked at the door, causing it to open wider. "If you're really here to put some coins on the coffers, then by all means come slip inside this house."

He turned his back on them, walking deeper into the house. He and Corey the PI exchanged a look. His companion shrugged and gave him an encouraging smile as he stepped into the long shadow cast forth from the dim entranceway, beckoning for him to follow. The same chemical smell from the joint permeated the interior hallway, only stronger, the air and walls fully saturated. There were other scents competing with it; strong incense, cigarette smoke, marijuana, dust, mold, animal excrement. Beyond the entrance hall there was a high-ceilinged room with four doors leading to various smaller rooms and a massive oak stairway in the center rising up to a second floor. Wheel slouched into the first door on the right. It was tough to see through the cloud of smoke and dust emanating from the room, the weasel's white fur acting as a beacon in the din for them to follow.

"Hey guys, Wesley Snipes and Zach Braff are here to pay off some random rich-ass junkie's debt."

Wheel announced this to the two individuals who were seated upon a battered leather couch that was most likely really expensive and chic just a decade or so previous. Sunk into the ripped cushion on the right side of the couch was a wiry young man with white jeans tucked into Doc Martin boots with white laces. He wore a tight black tee exposing arm sleeve tats of various harsh-looking symbols including at least one swastika. His head was shaved, and there was an intricate spider web inked above his left ear. He smirked as they entered while noisily cracking his neck. Next to him was an even skinnier young man with a mass of corkscrew dreadlocks tied up in a bright green bandana, He was barefoot and clad in baggy jeans that were visibly filthy. A multitude of colored bracelets lined his wrists, each bearing a slogan such as *Meat Is Murder* and *1 World, 1 People*. The kid was perched on the edge of the couch and was smiling at them expectantly as if about to be introduced to some old friends of Wheel's he had heard so much about.

"Well, well, look at this," Corey the PI said, nodding to the dreadlocked kid and the skinhead,. "All hands across the world. Inspiring, really. Hiya fellas."

As his eyes adjusted to the dim, dank interior the room came into better focus. A coffee table littered with smartphones, lighters, rolls of tinfoil, a Cream album (*Wheels Of Fire*) with a mound of buds and rolling papers on it. A massive flat screen with the Netflix logo glowing in red, sitting atop an upturned peach crate. Posters on the walls: The Grateful Dead, young and laughing on a porch; Peter Tosh peeking out from a field of marijuana plants; Janis Joplin grinning broadly and holding a bottle of Southern Comfort. There was a movement in the far corner of the room. A green easy chair which had been facing the wall spun to reveal a barrel-chested young man with peroxide-blond, close-cropped hair and a pair of overalls with no shirt on underneath. His eyes were rolled back into their sockets and his head was slumped on the cushion. In his lap sat a small girl with straight blond hair parted in the middle, '70s-style, barefoot with cutoff jean shorts and a tee that bore the slogan *War In Peace*. She regarded them with a feral look, her chin downturned. He squinted hard. Yes, there in the corner next to the chair, glinting red from the television screen, was a long sword resting against the wall within the girl's reach.

He thought of the pod, the controlled space, the filtered air. His paradise felt miles away in the midst of all this squalor and disorder. Wheel sat down atop a yellow Moroccan ottoman. The little white beast leapt down onto his knee.

"So fate has brought you to our door this fine morning."

He finished off the joint in one long pull. The weasel perked its head in expectation as Wheel bent down to gently, lovingly, blow smoke into its face.

"Let's get down to our dirty deeds, shall we? Hey Piss!"

He looked to the large dude in the overalls who remained passed out in the lazy boy. A strung out Assyrian king passed out on his throne. The girl had not broken her glare. Piss didn't budge.

"Just cut to the chase, Wheelie. These men bring bad vibes," the kid with the dreads said in an improve night Jamaican accent. He held a jar between his thighs and was carefully sprinkling something onto a piece of tin foil. "Besides, today might get hectic, don't forget.

"Oh, *we* bring bad vibes? Ok, then, Kale," Corey the PI said cheerfully. "Then let's indeed get this done and let you guys get back to your....thing. As I said before, we've come to pay off a debt. Their names are Jennifer, Samantha, and Chlorinde. Some SUNY chicks? Surely those names ring a bell since you've been putting feelers out on them for a month."

Wheel's face betrayed no sense of recognition or feeling. He dropped the end of the laced joint which had been smoldering far too close to his fingers, the weasel happily breathing in the fumes, into an empty can of Austin Eastenders Cider on the coffee table.

"The amount is one thousand dollars, even, owed to you for an ounce of weed and a dozen capsules of molly," Corey the PI spoke in a business-like tone. He pulled an envelope from his back pocket with the cash he had withdrawn from an ATM in the lobby of the pod hotel the day previous. "Plus an extra two hundo for the late payment fee."

Wheel was gently petting the weasel's head, nodding to himself as the kid Corey the PI had just identified as Kale flicked a lighter underneath the foil, sucking in the fumes through a long tube. He was watching the sword, hoping the girl with the feral stare wouldn't reach for it. Kale sat back with the smoldering foil still in his hand, grinning dumbly. The skinhead took the foil from his hand in a motherly manner, placing it carefully back on the table.

"Surely you know those three." Corey the PI kept a laser focus on Wheel, who continued nodding and petting the weasel.

"Oh yea I know em'," Wheel admitted. "SUNY thots. Looking to party. Dime-a-dozen."

"That's one of their Dads," Corey the PI pointed to him.

Kale giggled at this, twisting a long dread between his fingers. The skinhead smirked, staring at the Netflix screen.

"Sorry, man," Wheel said respectfully, a slight hint of up-standing North Jersey upbringing showing through in his tone. "But the world needs to realize it isn't about the debt. A thousand bags of sand? I could really give a fuck, to be honest. It's about these college priveys, bruh. They don't appreciate *the struggle*. They have the cash but would never dream of funneling it to the underclass. Not even when they owe it. I'll send Piss out to knock off a Starbucks and make that in ten minutes. Speaking of which, Fawn, wake that dude up will you, babe?"

Without taking her eyes off of them, Fawn gave Piss three quick jabs to the rib with her elbow. He opened his eyes, panicked, looking to the TV. "Hey what happened to *Lock Up Raw?*"

"Pissy, we have *visitors*," Wheel called out in sing-song.

"The struggle?" Corey the PI shook his head. "You grew up in a 2.2 million dollar suburban home in a top ten school district. You had your own bathroom as a child. The only reason you went to a state school is that juvenile felony battery charge senior year in high school…"

The girl's void-embracing grin had grown wider. Piss shifted to focus on them, his eyes clouding slowly with fury.

"C Man," he hissed out the side of his mouth to his new partner. "Just hand over the cash. You're antagonizing them. Worst PI ever."

Wheel appeared to be enjoying the situation immensely, an underworld circus announcer allowing the shots to call themselves.

"My mans here has done his *homework* on me, Sam," he spoke to the weasel in a soothing tone, grinning to reveal the set of platinum gnashers on display in the photo he had seen.

"Ok, regardless of the various class structure and socio-political issues highlighted in this scenario, the simple fact of the matter is that Jennifer, Samantha, and Chlorinde owe you a grand plus interest in good old fashioned soon-to-be-worthless USD," Corey the PI said in a rush, holding out the envelope. "And here it is. So you can stop sending your townie cult members to harass them in the cafeteria line. Do we or don't we have a deal?"

Strained giggling from Kale as he held his hands over his face, rocking back and forth.

"But maybe I enjoy harassing my former peoples far more than gaining a little cash off this petty-ass deal," Wheel spoke clearly in a low register, his agitation increasing. The weasel in his lap appeared worried, scrunching back its ears and rocking its head from side to side. "That one band means nothing to me. Absolutely nothing, What *does* mean something to me is *respect*. Those kids at that school need to know The Wheel can't be fucked with. Ya see, a wheel is round and is the completion of all things, plus it allows movement, progress, but it can also be *dangerous*. It can roll you right over. Crush your head. Smash your legs. Leave you cut in half on the road. If those kids don't know that, I'm fucked here in my business, ya see? If they think they can skip out on debts and get their Daddy to pay if the heat gets too much. If I let one get away with it, then they'll all try. I learned this in Intro To Business. Right there at their very own school, man. It's a message from brand to consumer. If you play out the Wheel, then the dorm maintenance man just might set your room on fire. It's pretty simple, really."

Piss was wide awake by now and was studying their two visitors with a bemused expression, his arm draped over Fawn's slight, slouched shoulders.

"At least two SUNY janitors live right here on this block," Piss interjected, his voice guttural from his long nap.

Corey the PI ignored him, keeping his focus on Wheel.

"Why does every dealer learn their shit from Freshman Biz 101," he wondered out loud. "It's as guaranteed as the sunrise."

Wheel sneered at this, menacingly flashing his grill. He could feel the blood beginning to churn in the base of his stomach. This wasn't going to be the easy handoff Corey had promised, the simple business transaction. For some reason the dig about Freshman business classes had increased the tense aura surrounding Wheel, who was a clear conduit for the vibe of the entire house. If Wheel felt it, they all felt it.

"Oh, the sunrise is *never* guaranteed, my friend," he said.

A movement to their left. Fawn had risen silently at some point and had the sword in her hands, taking on a convincing battle stance. Piss rose from the chair behind her, at least six-foot-three, one strap on his overalls hanging loose. The skinhead rose as well, his eyes on Wheel and the weasel, waiting for instruction. More demented giggling from Kale who was now spread prostrate on the leather couch with a pillow over his head. The beast and its owner stayed seated on the ottoman, not taking their eyes off the visitors.

He wished he could teleport himself outside to one of the overgrown parks he had seen lining the desolate townscape, green shards of a long-fallen empire. Anything to not be in this particular situation. He would gladly take his place on the municipal benches with the borderline homeless and the mentally unstable and the rest of the denizens of the void, staring straight ahead forevermore.

Several muffled thumps sounded from the back of the room, each one sending cascading ripples through his body that lifted him onto his toes. They came from behind a large scale Jim Morrison poster on the back wall of the room. The thuds caused Morrison's confident smirk to shudder and quake. The corner of the poster fell, revealing a door behind it.

In action movies the intruders always come crashing through with one kick that sends the door flying off its hinges. It took the real life intruders nine repeated kicks. The first kick their hosts hadn't noticed. The second and third had them exchanging confused glances. Kale finally removed his hands from his face. "I *told you* today would get hectic." By the fifth kick everyone was facing the door. Wheel had risen as well. "Be safe, Sam." He placed the weasel on the ground and watched longingly as the beast zigzagged out of the room. Fawn had turned the sword toward Jim Morrison. The skinhead was reaching around in the couch cushions, swearing, until he found what he was looking for: a large, gleaming handgun. He had never been in such close presence of a gun before. He backed away slightly, afraid, but nobody else in the room was paying him any mind. Corey the PI had his eyes on Piss, who kicked over the lazy boy to reveal a long rifle on the floor which he scooped up and held aloft in one graceful motion. On the eighth kick the PI sighed and, even though it looked as if he didn't want to, pulled a smaller handgun from the waste of his jeans. An aluminum bat had at some point materialized in Wheel's hands. Even Kale, who remained on the couch with his head slumped, muttering "I knew they were coming. I knew they were coming. I knew they were...", had produced a nasty-looking dagger from somewhere with wolf eyes on the handle. He realized he was the only person in the room without a weapon. Wheel winked at him, clearly excited as the pounding on the door continued. He searched the table, coming up with an empty beer bottle with a Dutch label.

Previously at odds, the hosts and visitors were allied now against whatever force was about to come in.

"Who's coming, Kale? Who's coming?" Corey the PI was shouting, crouched in a shooter's stance next to Piss, each with their weapon trained on the back door. Kale didn't have time to answer, for on the ninth kick a boot came through Jim Morrison's right knee. They watched as the foot struggled to remove itself. Then a hand came through, feeling for the lock. It took him a moment to find it.

"Oh man," Kale kept giggling. "Oh man."

Finally the door opened. A short, late-20s man with blue eyes sporting a white gown-type garment and boots. The designated door kicker. He wore a bulging wool cap that could barely contain his mounds of dreadlocks. Behind him were two taller men in Adidas tracksuits, both caucasian and in their 30s and with their dreads hanging loose. The older, taller men, both wielding fire axes, were laughing at the clumsiness of the door kicker, who had a wooden baseball bat. It took them a moment for their eyes to adjust to the inner darkness, standing in the harsh sunlight with an overgrown yard spread out behind them.

They froze when they saw the people, the guns, the swords, the knives, their eyes bulging. They had clearly not planned on being outnumbered.

"Good afternoon, Goat," Wheel said genially. "I take it you're here because you think we burned your field down. But newsflash, dude, it wasn't us."

"We weren't expecting an army, Wheelie," one of the track suit men said, moving his eyes across all the individuals in the house. "Who's the guy with the bottle though? Hope you got a discount on that one."

Suddenly a room full of armed lunatics was looking at him. He placed the bottle back on the table. He felt ridiculous.

"These two are with us."

Wheel gestured at him and Corey the PI with the bat.

"Isn't that right," he asked out the side of his mouth, not taking his eyes off the intruders.

"I guess we are are now," Corey the PI shrugged, his gun trained on the little guy in the white tunic.

"And isn't that right, Hero Dad?"

He realized Wheel was speaking to him.

"Yea, I guess," he said, not knowing what to do with his hands.

"That crop was our food for the year, brother," the short one said, his nostrils flaring, glaring in the direction of the couch.

"Kale! I knew it! You used to be *one of us*! Like a son and a brother rolled into one!"

Rocking back and forth with dagger in hand, Kale kept up a chant.

"Here they are. Here they are. Here they are," he whispered. "Three wise men, cometh across the desert to see thy newly born king."

"Shut it, Kale," Wheel instructed before addressing their visitors once more.

"Look man, nobody here had anything to do with torching your little field. We're of no threat to you. We full believe in a free market."

"Business 101!" Corey the PI shouted, cutting him off. The visitors turned to him, seemingly less frightened than they should have been by the weapon he had trained on them.

"Look, I don't know what kind of obscure vendetta is going down here, but my mans and I aren't a part of it. Let us walk."

Corey the PI was pointing at him. The little door kicker grinned.

"The only ones that walk are these three shag heaps," Wheel said, smirking at their visitors. "Walk all the way back to their smoldering field. Unless they want to get murked up in here."

All three intruders grinned defiantly.

"Ain't nobody gettin' murked but yourself, friend," one of the tall track suit men said in a determined purr. "We'll take all those toys from you like nothing. Startin' with you, honey."

The tall intruder took a step toward Fawn, who stood her ground with her sword. There was a movement from the couch, Kale rising and standing with his arms outstretched, his eyes wild.

"I'm the one who torched it, Goat," he said proudly. "And when you grow it back up, I'll torch it again. Oh yes. Oh yes. Again and again and again and…"

When he tried to envision it later, he would see it all happening in slow motion and bright focus, each action bathed in clear light. In reality, the whole thing went down in less than a minute and was as garbled and confused as a film from a warped projector.

The man Kale had referred to as "Goat" stealthily kicked Fawn's legs out from under her, grabbing the sword by the handle as she fell. His tall partner kicked the end of Piss's rifle, causing it to smack off the top of his head with a sickening thwack, knocking him to the floor. Now the two elder intruding white Rastas had a sword and a rifle and were advancing on the rest.

It was then that the weasel named Samantha reappeared, leaping down from a high shelf where she had been hiding and landing on Goat's head, screeching wildly. Goat yelled out, trying to shake her off, but Samantha had her teeth and claws dug hard into the top of his skull. In the commotion he had dropped the sword. Fawn scrambled over the unconscious Piss to get to it. The white rasta with the rifle had his weapon trained on Corey the PI, but he was distracted by Goat's screams. Coming up behind him, grinning dementedly, Fawn brought the sword down with expert precision, taking off the white rasta's left earlobe. He sank to his knees, yelling gibberish. The rifle dropped from his hands, hitting the floor with a deafening BOOM.

He didn't know whether to duck or jump. Corey the PI hit the deck, as did Wheel and the skinhead. Kale was twirling in place, lost in some sort of shaman dance. Bits of plaster rained from above. The bullet had gone through the ceiling. Goat rose to his feet, the weasel still attached to his head, entangled in his dreadlocks now, and ran through the busted door into the back yard, screaming as if being skinned alive. Fawn had the short intruder in the white tunic up against the wall at sword-point.

"Look, honey, they said they'd give me fifty bucks to kick a door in. That's all this was supposed to be," he was saying, his hands in the air.

A movement below him. The other tracksuit man, blood dripping down the side of his face from the spot where his earlobe used to be, was crawling toward the rifle. He moved for it too, getting there before his opponent, placing his foot on it so he couldn't pick it up.

It was an instinctual move that surprised him greatly even as it was happening, adapting to the violence like all else. What he overlooked in that moment was the knife the man had pulled from the bottom cuff of the tracksuit. He would have happily plunged it through his foot had Corey the PI not sprung from the floor with his gun.

"Drop it!"

For a moment all was silent but Kale's chanting as he twirled around the destroyed room, the upturned furniture, the swirling plaster, the blood. Wheel soon joined him, stiffly mimicking his snaking hip dance, waving the bat dangerously.

"This is why I'm here," he yelled with great conviction. "I've crossed over and I'm never going back!"

He realized there was nothing between him and the front door. He began backing toward it. There was a sound from in front of the house. Oh God, what now? Out the window he saw the Suburban, with Brig at the wheel, driving up onto the lawn and making its way toward the front door. It struck him that all of this was happening in broad daylight in a residential neighborhood. Corey the PI, Fawn, and the skinhead were backing the tall, bloody tracksuit man and his door kicker friend in the white tunic out the busted back door at gun-knife-and-sword-point. Samantha the weasel had returned from outside and was safely atop Wheel's shoulder. A dreadlock clump hung from her mouth.

"I think you boys better be running along now," Corey the PI said to the battered and stunned intruders. "And if you come back, we got more ferrets or whatever waiting for your asses."

They all watched as the two of them pulled Goat, who had been laying in the back yard, to his feet. They ran full speed into the wooden fence that separated Wheel's yard from the neighbors, bringing down the entire section with them. The last they saw them they were running across the neighbor's yard, their tracksuits and white gown stained with blood.

"Samantha is a *weasel*," Wheel corrected him.

Kale danced out into the sun behind them, his arms outstretched as if cleansing the humid air, letting out little whoops. The dagger was still clutched in his hand. There were voices, excited and confused, coming from the other yards, from the houses, from the street.

"We better clear out this bitch before the Kingston PD rolls up." Corey the PI backed up to him, placing the gun in his belt. "That shot was loud, man."

Wheel was shouting out benevolent orders that sounded more like questions, the weasel with its claws dug into his shirt trying to hang on. He had bits of ceiling plaster in his hair.

"We may have some heat coming in, my peoples. Let's get this house clear, shall we?"

His crew was soon scampering into other rooms, up the stairs, their faces determined. Kale continued his snake dance in the yard.

"Thanks for the assistance today." Wheel sauntered over to where they were standing by the door. "Who says you can't make new friends in the modern world?"

Corey the PI waved his hand dismissively.

"You're not going to be seeing us again," he told him with definite finality. "Friends for twenty minutes."

He dug the envelope with the cash out of his back pocket. It was surprising he had held onto it through the entire melee.

"Friends of the Devil," Wheel said, flashing his platinum teeth.

He took the envelope. He and the weasel regarded them expectantly.

"So we're all set?"

Wheel looked to Samantha before nodding reluctantly.

"Yea, we're good."

He let the bat drop to the scuffed hardwood. He looked him full on, his clouded blue eyes emanating something close to compassion, a considerate host in the midst of a whirlwind household.

"The only people worth their own lives are those of us on a quest," he said with a slight bow.

They were back at Brig's residence, safe inside his massive garage. Corey the PI was in the process of changing the license plate on the Suburban, choosing one from a stack he kept in the back. Brig was worried his wife would come home early, and the two of them were bickering without much venom.

Earlier Brig had backed quickly down the long strip of dead lawn outside Wheel's residence as neighbors began coming out of their houses on either side, standing on their porches, confused by the screaming, the loud bangs, the gunshot. Brig had backed over one of the neighbor's birdfeeders in their escape. His hands didn't stop shaking until the vehicle pulled onto the onramp that would take them out of Kingston proper.

"I really thought you two were dead in there, man," he said, standing with his arms crossed while Corey the PI screwed on the new plate. The whole thing was going south from the moment you walked in. Figured I'd pull up for the big escape, but to be honest I wasn't sure you'd both make it out."

The two of them embraced, thumping each other loudly on the back.

"Pod Man here is a lucky talisman."

Brig smirked at this.

"Yea, well the lucky talisman owes me five hundred."

"I got you," he assured him. "Like I said, there'll be a check in the mail shortly."

He nodded, arching his eyebrows.

"Just another thing to compartmentalize," he said.

The three of them sat in a classic rock-themed coffee shop on a street off the main strip in New Paltz. Him, Corey the PI, and Jennifer. He had phoned her as they approached the town. She hadn't sounded surprised to get a call from him out of nowhere, or by the fact that that he was in town and out of the pods for some mysterious reason, but since seating herself at the table under a massive framed shot of The Band standing in a snow-covered field, she did appear bewildered. It made him suspicious that she could just meet them like this at the spur of the moment. Shouldn't she be in class? But he was very glad to see her. She looked terrific, with strikingly clear skin and her hair pulled back sloppily, in jeans and a white top with intricate straps keeping it afloat.

"Dad, why are you rolling with cops?" She nodded to Corey the PI, who sipped his latte and grinned at the accusation.

"This is my good friend Corey."

He left it at that.

"I appreciate the stop-through, but I can't be long," she said. "I have to cram for a test and need to figure out whose room to crash in tonight…"

"That's not going to be a problem anymore, honey," Corey the PI said, winking at her.

She looked to him, then to her father, wide eyed.

He had expected a variety of questions, badgering and childish. But Jennifer was no longer a child. At some point she'd become discreet and intuitive.

"I guess I don't even want to know," she said.

He realized in the moment she made this statement that she would be just fine.

"Oh, you *definitely* don't," he assured her.

Standing with Jennifer on the narrow sidewalk outside the coffee shop. Two massive Bob Dylan prints lined each window. Across the street was a bookstore called "Feed Your Head" which was situated next to a headshop named "Fourth Eye". Corey the PI was waiting by the parked Suburban, affording them a moment of privacy.

"Jesus, Dad, I'm impressed. This whole pod trip has you straightened right out. You even look different."

She paused.

"I guess what I'm trying to say is 'thank you'."

He waved away her gratitude.

"Just no more dealings with white rasta neo-gangster fringe townies with killer weasels, ok?"

She nodded affirmative.

"So what are you going to do about Mom? The house? Your world?"

A tinge of real emotion bled through in her words, the first she had displayed since his run for the pods.

"I'll let you get to your studies."

With a quick step forward, she threw her arms around him. The hug was brief but the squeeze was very tight, as if he was hot and could burn her if she wasn't quick enough.

They passed her on the strip as they were driving. They didn't honk or shout. She was walking with her arms folded, her head held high as if drinking in the breeze.

Half-an-hour later they were well out of Ulster County, passing through the numbing open spaces in the sprawl north of the city. They hadn't spoken a word in the past ten minutes . The radio wasn't on. Corey the PI was looking thoughtfully ahead, pushing the Suburban just over the speed limit in the light traffic. Finally he spoke.

"Has it ever occurred to you that those two precipice point cult people never existed?"

Earlier, just after they had left New Paltz, Corey the PI had asked about the source for his transition to the pods. He had told him the entire story in a rush, but it hadn't sounded as grand and all-encompassing out loud, in the open air, as it had to him as it was happening.

"I do know that."

Corey the PI nodded mournfully at this. It occurred to him that they were fast approaching the second of the three exits that would have taken him to his and Catharine's house.

"You know, my whole job centers around snatching back airborne souls," he said. "People with too little to weigh them down. They get caught up in the winds. I guess you'd call it chaos. They can't harness it or use it to their advantage. They can't compartmentalize. They get swept out."

He looked him dead on, keeping one hand on the wheel.

"You're gonna' haunt me for a long time, my friend. The guy who *wanted* to be swept out. The guy who sought the winds in order to harness chaos. He didn't find a lover. He didn't clean out an account at work and vanish. He didn't take 42 Klonopin and a warm motel bath."

The day had exhausted him. The violence. The long stretch spent in the crippling failure of the world beyond the pods. The onset of confusion throwing off hard-won convictions.

"Un-fucking-believable," Corey the PI was whispering as they approached the next exit. He eased into the slow lane, letting his foot off the gas a little.

"So what should I do," he asked.

The green rectangular sign. The white letters. The cloudless, sunny skies. The yellow road lines. The vastness. The vacuum. The barriers. The obscure systems. The unspoken oaths. The balance controls. The sectioned-off lives. The dimensions bleeding into others. The hundreds of thousands of tiny empires. Thriving. Failing. Combining and combusting. The shifting peripheries. The half-opened gates. The battles against the dusts.

"Don't take the exit," he said.

About the Author

Daniel Falatko is the author of two previous novels, *Condominium* (CCLAP, 2014) and *Travels & Travails Of Small Minds* (Ardent Press, 2017). His music writing can be found on niche-appeal.com. A graduate of the MFA in Creative Writing program at Vermont College, he lives, writes, and works in New York City.

www.ingramcontent.com/pod-product-compliance
Lightning Source LLC
Chambersburg PA
CBHW020023030726
47499CB00007B/2253